TALL ORDER

•

Constance Sprague

AVALON BOOKS
NEW YORK

© Copyright 2005 by Constance Sprague
Library of Congress Catalog Card Number: 2004098740
ISBN 0-8034-9712-1
Published by Thomas Bouregy & Co., Inc.
160 Madison Avenue, New York, NY 10016

PRINTED IN THE UNITED STATES OF AMERICA
ON ACID-FREE PAPER
BY HADDON CRAFTSMEN, BLOOMSBURG, PENNSYLVANIA

This book is for Lily, Mike and Aleta,
who taught me everything
I know about drama, irony and style.

Chapter One

Slashing her red pencil savagely through the words scribbled in the blanks Ava noticed two girls snoring softly at their desks in the back row and she thought bitterly that the real problem with art history wasn't that it was boring or irrelevant but that it lacked firepower. A few well timed cherry bombs would work wonders with this class.

"And that's why you can see here, from this chiaroscuro, that Gentileschi was strongly influenced by Caravaggio." At the slide screen in front of the class Dora Grant droned on like a docent in the National Gallery, and Ava winced at the nasal whine of her voice. No wonder the class fell asleep. And Dora, God bless her, was probably the only student in the entire class who actually cared deeply about art. It really wasn't her fault that she was NyQuil personified.

"Thank you Dora for that well-researched presentation. I'm afraid we don't have time enough for anyone else to give their project today, so we'll just end a little early and continue on Wednesday," Ava slammed a book on her desk and smiled bleakly as several of the students leapt in their seats. The class stirred from its torpor and shuffled out like the living dead with backpacks.

Ava sat in the empty room smelling the chalk dust and

1

struggled to suppress the feeling that her own life was being erased. She stuffed her books into her own backpack and trudged out into the hall where eager yapping students bustled past, all of them quite convinced apparently that they were destined for lives filled with meaning, adventure, romance. Ava remembered when she had believed in such things. It wasn't so long ago. She didn't believe in them anymore. Except possibly the romance. She hadn't lost all hope yet, anyway.

Crunch, crunch, crunch, crunch. The next morning the beat of her Nikes on the cinder path pounded a counter-rhythm to the Eurythmics song stuck in Ava's head. She moved smoothly, her limbs long and loose. No thoughts in her head but the clear purpose of training for the marathon. Some people get centered through yoga, or meditation; Ava found her center in motion. Ever since she was twelve years old, Ava had found solace in the discipline of competitive running. She liked the paradox of a solitary activity that could be experienced while surrounded by a pack of like-minded heavy breathing strangers.

Ava circled the park, enjoying the frosty air, watching the pigeons scatter and settle back as she passed. She put on a burst of speed as she came to the last stretch, the straightaway to the parking lot where her dark blue Toyota waited. Coming abreast of the car Ava reached into the pocket of her hooded sweatshirt for her keys and her heart skipped in panic. No keys. Nothing. Nada.

She looked back at the jogging path and wondered how far back they might be. Usually the jingle of her keys played like a mini-tambourine as she ran. Funny, she hadn't noticed them falling out. She shook her head and looked at her watch. *Oh my God,* she thought. *Eight-fifteen! How did I zone out so badly?*

She had to get to her class by 9. No time to run back and look for the keys. Frantically, Ava retraced the last hundred feet of the path anyway, hoping against the odds that she might find them. The frozen grass glittered, teasing her, turning every odd stone into a glinting possibility. Giving up the hunt after several frustrating minutes, Ava realized if she ran all the way she might just make it back to her apartment in time to change.

But, how was she going to get in her apartment? Spare key. Chenille had her spare key. By now Ava was jogging down Monument, her thoughts racing ahead of her, figuring how she could get into her apartment, change quickly into her work clothes, and then . . . somehow, find time to swing by Starbucks. No matter how late she might be, coffee was non-negotiable.

Sometimes Ava thought her life would be simpler if she could just get a caffeine patch. Forget worrying about spilling hot cups of coffee, forget finding time to grab a cup between classes. Just absorb it like sunshine directly into her system.

But, as she stood in line a short while later at the Starbucks on Center Avenue listening to the soothing hiss of the espresso machine, the comforting roar of the milk foamer, the satin voice of Ella Fitzgerald on the music system, she reflected, *This is why a patch wouldn't work. I need context in my fix.*

A coffee addict long before the Starbucks franchise spread like a rash across the nation, Ava Morrison was drinking homemade lattes before the term developed commercial cache. Raised in a household with a French mother and a military father, Ava grew up expecting a pitcher of warm milk to accompany the morning caffé, and she was amused the first time she heard about the so-called Seattle coffee renaissance with its "invention" of the latte.

In Ava's experience, which included her father's tours of duty in Panama and El Salvador, Americans had been kind of slow to branch out into the dark, exotic, and altogether addictive coffee world. Still, she mused, examining the menu board offering its bewildering array of double mocha frappuccinos, short grandes and the like, better late than never.

Today, Ava's cup was scented with cinnamon and contained a booster rocket of double espresso. It was going to be a long day. She fished her sunglasses out of her bag, pulled her Polartec cap down over her hair, and hurried out into the sharp February sunshine. She wasn't looking forward to this next class. Intro to Art History always attracted a high percentage of students who enrolled because they thought it would be an easy class, and it was Ava's unpleasant duty to correct this assumption, which inevitably meant reading piles of ill-considered and dubiously researched papers. Sometimes Ava wanted to set a match to the lot.

Instead she gritted her teeth, inhaled her coffee and grimly forged ahead. In her darkest hours she blamed her father for instilling her with the dogged work ethic of a Marine. But, like Colonel Hank Morrison, she took pride in doing her job, even if it wasn't the job she had dreamed of as a little girl.

That dream job, which only her best friend Chenille knew she still dreamed about, was to be an actress. Not a superstar like Meg Ryan or Nicole Kidman. Ava knew she didn't have that kind of cute spunky thing or that brittle beauty. But she did have something, she just knew it. For one thing, she could memorize lines and speak them with intelligence and feeling. And this was not something everyone could do, Ava knew. Her mother, Ariel, had read poetry and literature to Ava all during her childhood, and Ava adored the way her mother could bring words to life. Ava secretly believed she had inherited her mother's verbal gift, if not her physical grace.

But, both her parents had discouraged Ava from pursuing a career in theatre. Her father expressed the view that theatre was frivolous and an unworthy pursuit for someone as smart as Ava. Her mother, usually so gracious, had been more harshly blunt. "Ava, you are much too tall to be an actress. No leading lady can be as tall as you, dear. And you don't want to be a character actress. They only get laughed at."

Ava had already been laughed at enough in grade school, when she broke the five-foot barrier well before anyone else her age, and later, even worse, in high school, when she finished her growth spurt at six-foot-one. And, no, she didn't like basketball, didn't play basketball, and grew to despise anyone who asked her if she did. And almost everyone who met her for the first time did.

So, she didn't try out for any of the high school drama productions. She found solace in art class, but her ability in the visual arts was modest at best. By her sophomore year in college a career in art history seemed the path of least resistance. Now, at twenty-seven, she was a teaching assistant at Virginia Commonwealth University and reasonably content, considering she lived alone and had only gone out on six dates in the last six years.

This, according to Chenille Montgomery, her best, and if Ava were honest, only real friend, was criminal and downright unhealthy.

"Honey, it's just not natural to go without for so long," Chenille asserted. This was a central tenet of the gospel of Chenille, which held that there was no problem in life which love couldn't solve. In other circumstances, Ava might have avoided someone like Chenille, with her honey blonde hair, large slightly bulging blue eyes and adorable smile, figuring that anyone so attractive couldn't understand how it felt to feel awkward in your own skin. But they became friends when they were undergrads together at William and Mary, in part because Chenille was just naturally nicer than most other people. She looked like she could be a spokesmodel for some children's cereal, but she was totally sympathetic to Ava's life in the tall lane, since Chenille knew the frustration of being typecast as a dumb blonde all her life.

When Chenille got hired by the VCU English Department Ava's life took a turn for the better, and now, with Chenille egging her on, Ava was about to try something for which she'd been waiting her whole life. Tucked in behind the freshman essays on the Baroque and Rococo periods, was a flyer announcing auditions for a local community theatre production of *Midsummer Night's Dream*. And Ava already knew Titania's entrance speech by heart.

All that morning at the drafting table in his Cary Street studio Troy Burnett tried without success to fit fish into a box. The small box on the graph paper represented the last remaining unoccupied space in the tiny row house yard of one of his best clients. Mrs. Ashley Trevor had her heart set on a koi pond. And though Troy had tried to talk her out of it, arguing that perhaps she should be content with the gazebo, the rock garden waterfall, the rose-covered pergola and the formal herb knot garden surrounded by miniature box topiary, he had failed. Nevermind that her total garden space was smaller than the average suburban rec room. Her rival in the Crestwood Garden Club had apparently installed a koi pond last summer and Mrs. Trevor was not about to be outdone.

Troy tore up another sheet of graph paper and tossed it toward the already overflowing bin. The ball of paper bounced off the basket and caught the attention of Simon, curled up in a bar of sunlight under the table. Simon sprang into action, chased the wad of paper across the oak floor, batting it with his paws until it disappeared under the couch. Then Simon sat on his haunches and gazed at Troy with a look of complete satisfaction.

Troy sighed. Cats made it look so easy. Troy was never satisfied with his own efforts. He found it easier to forgive the mistakes of others than his own, and right about now he was beginning to think that entering the dirty business of landscape design had been a big mistake. Maybe his father had been right. Maybe he should have stuck with engineering. Then he wouldn't have to deal with all these fussy women with their grandiose ideas and their suburban limitations.

He glanced up at the bulletin board above his table, crowded with photos and sketches of gardens, each one reminding him of what it was he loved about his work— creating beautiful settings, living art, working with light and shadow, being outside. *That's what I need*, he thought. *I've got to get outside.* This long dreary winter had put a strain on his spirit and his bank account, but now, at least, the days were getting longer. Soon it would be March. The planting season would begin, and he knew he'd be glad he wasn't stuck in some office doing calculus. Plus, Josh's soccer season would kick off soon, and watching his son play soccer gave Troy almost more joy than doing it himself.

But, this spring would also be different than any other because for the first time in his life, Troy had a play to direct in the community theatre. And that was another way of creating settings, making live art, working with light and shadow. His jock buddies didn't understand why he loved theatre work. He'd given up trying to make them understand. After all, outside of the soccer field, Troy didn't have much in common with the rest of his teammates, except for Carlos, his right hand man in the business and on the team.

Carlos had been divorced longer than Troy, and had reached the stage when he was beginning to look for new love. With the enthusiasm of a new convert, Carlos was always trying to get Troy to meet some woman or other. Troy didn't want to hear it. What he wanted was what he thought he'd found with his ex-wife. True love.

Hah. He smiled ruefully to think what a sap he'd been. He and Kerry began dating their senior year in high school, and Troy could hardly believe how lucky he was, dating a cheerleader, one of the most popular girls in school. And when she stuck with him all through college, he thought they must be made for each other. Of course, he was surprised when she got pregnant while he was in his sophomore year. But he was only too happy to marry her, and everything seemed fine right up until he graduated. Things began to get bad as soon as he started his own business. The going was slow and the money even slower at first, and Kerry had little patience. She wanted a house, an SUV, vacations at Disneyworld. Troy struggled to keep up, but before he even managed to get them out of the condo Kerry had begun spending her free time with a hunky mechanic who, Troy soon learned, was tuning up more than her engine.

His emotions blunted with shock, Troy got through the divorce without ever losing his temper. Somehow, he'd always known that Kerry was too pretty, too popular to be with him. Troy agreed to share custody of Josh, offering to keep his son every weekend, an arrangement that suited Kerry's social calendar just perfectly. Troy was so wounded by the betrayal that he couldn't even imagine wanting to go out with another woman, so he was happy to spend all his free time with his three-year-old son.

Four years later, little had changed in Troy's life. Except that his business was now a solid success. His "Pocket Garden" designs had won him a huge and loyal following in the greater Richmond area. And now that Josh was older he could even take him along when he had weekend work. But, lately, even when his seven-year-old son was with him, Troy found his eye wandering whenever an attractive woman was near. He felt the emptiness more keenly in the apartment whenever Josh left. But he couldn't see how he could balance the needs of his son with his own. So, instead, Troy concentrated on trying keep his weekends free, not just for Josh, but for theatre work.

Troy couldn't even begin to explain why he loved theatre the way he did. Certainly he'd never been exposed to it very much growing up in Virginia Beach. He and his sister had been encouraged to play sports, and musical instruments, but that was it. His father, an electrician, and his mother, a hairdresser, considered going to the theatre something rich people did. But in college Troy had enrolled in a drama class on impulse and he'd been amazed at how much fun it was. Plus, the people were so much more friendly and open-minded than he'd expected. And Troy discovered he had a natural talent for creating sets.

Troy had set aside his theatre hobby when he first came to Richmond with Kerry. He'd had to concentrate on getting his business established. But now, finally, he felt he could allow himself the luxury of getting involved in one of the local community theatres. When he saw the small notice of the James River Players' call for directors in the *Times Dispatch* he called and got an application. He was excited about the auditions tonight. It would be his first time in the director's chair, but, at twenty-seven, he felt he was ready for the challenge. He just hoped some good people showed up for the auditions.

As the squealing hinges pierced the silent auditorium, Troy turned toward the entrance and saw silhouetted there a woman whose head nearly grazed the door frame. The door clanged shut behind her as she walked slowly down the aisle, stopping when she came to Troy's row.

He took in her short dark hair, her long nose, her VCU sweatshirt.

"You're trying out for Helena?" he asked, tapping a pen on the clipboard on his lap.

Ava pursed her lips slightly. "Is the part of Titania already cast?"

Troy felt the challenge in her tone. "No, nothing's been cast yet. I just thought . . ." He stopped, wary. He reached down beside his chair and grabbed a script and an audition form.

"Here, fill this out and let me know when you're ready to read."

Ava frowned. "Am I the only one here? The flyer said seven o'clock, I thought."

"That's right. No. You're on time. A lot of people probably have trouble getting here this early, coming from work or school." He paused, noticing her large wide-set eyes. "Do you work? Or are you a student?"

"Are those my only options?"

He smiled. "No, I hope not."

She smiled then, and he fell back against his seat. Maybe Titania wouldn't be a stretch, he thought.

"I'm a teacher. Ava Morrison. Art history." She reached

out her hand to shake his and a jolt of heat went up his arm as he touched her. She looked at him thoughtfully for a moment before releasing his hand.

She slid into a seat two down from his and began filling out the form. "You must be the director?"

"Yep."

"Do you do this for a living?"

"I wish. No, actually, I wouldn't want to do this for a living. I'd probably hate it if I did it full time." Troy paused, debating whether to tell her about his day job. But other people were starting to drift into the auditorium, so he decided to focus on the job at hand.

For the next ten minutes Troy was too busy handing out forms and answering questions to get down to work, but when the pace slackened he looked up, caught Ava's eye and said, "Since you were here first, would you like to start?"

Ava felt her heart speeding and stood up quickly. "Shall I go up on the stage?"

"Yes," replied Troy, looking not at Ava but at the entrance again, where the noisy door had just admitted another girl who was jogging down the aisle. When she reached Troy she held out her hand for an audition form and said breathlessly, "Hi. I have to get to a class at eight. Can I go first?"

Ava stared at the girl, who was pretty and short, her dark brown hair caught in a ponytail. Then Ava noticed Troy giving her an inquisitive look, and she felt him gauging her height with respect to the newcomer.

"Sure, go ahead," said Ava. After all, she didn't have any other plans for this evening, if you didn't count the stack of papers waiting to be graded, and Ava would rather not.

"Oh thanks," gushed the girl, throwing off her peacoat and scampering up on stage. When she got there she took a few seconds to compose herself and then announced. "I'm going to read for Hermia, okay?"

"Do you want someone to read the scene with you?" asked Troy, glancing over at Ava.

Ava could see it coming. He was already picturing her as

Helena, the tall girl, the geeky loser with a crush on Hermia's lover. Ava knew the part all too well, but she had no desire to play it. What was the point in acting if you had to relive the worst roles of your own life? She wanted to be Titania, Queen of the Fairies, regal, amorous, desirable. Ava felt like she'd been sandbagged.

"How about you," Troy looked down at the sheet Ava had filled in, "Ava? Would you read the part of Helena with, um . . . ?" He looked up at the girl on stage.

"Heather," she sang out.

Right, thought Ava. *You would be.*

"I really came prepared to try out for Titania," she began.

Troy nodded patiently. "Yes, I understand. You can read for that part too. But just to help Heather with her audition, could you read the part of Helena?"

Ava tried not to frown. Be a good sport, she told herself. A team player. She sighed and walked up on stage. Standing there next to Heather she knew how perfectly they fit the Mutt and Jeff dimensions of the roles. But surely there must be some other girl who wants to be Helena, she thought.

"Pick it up from Act Three, Scene two," said Troy.

Heather chirped into action as Hermia, accusing Helena, her "tall personage," of stealing her boyfriend, and Ava gamely read her lines, her heart sinking with each word. When they finished the quarreling scene they got a small round of applause.

"Thanks Heather, that was great." Troy was smiling at them both. "And Ava, I really hope you'll consider taking the part of Helena. I think you'd be good in it."

Ava twisted her lips in a tight smile and said, "If you don't mind, I'd still like to read for Titania."

"Sure, of course. Do you want to do that now? Or would you rather let some of the others go first?"

Ava hesitated. It was all happening so fast. Her pulse was still hammering from the humiliation of having to spar with Heather. "I'll wait till some of the others have had a chance."

"Fine," said Troy.

Ava returned to her seat and watched miserably for the next hour as various college kids and older adults read for the roles of Bottom, Puck, Lysander, and Demetrius. Four other women read for Titania. Three of them didn't worry Ava at all. They had no timing, no poetry, no passion. But the fourth woman, slightly older, with a head of fiery copper hair and eyes that flashed like a silent film star's, delivered the lines in a voice that gave Ava goosebumps. She was good. Really good. Ava tried to tell herself that she was as good as that woman, but she wasn't that good a liar. She sank back in her seat feeling defeated.

Then a tall broad shouldered man with auburn hair and perfect teeth stepped on the stage and said, " 'Ill met by moonlight proud Titania.' "

Ava's mouth dropped open and her breathing became quick and shallow as she listened to the man reciting the famous first speech by Oberon, King of the Fairies. *Oh, God*, thought Ava, watching him moving on the stage as if he'd been born there. *Please let me be his Titania.*

When the man finished the few people still in the auditorium applauded, and he took a smiling bow.

Then Ava was startled to hear the director calling her name. "Ava? Are you ready to give us your Titania now?"

She grabbed her script, even though she'd memorized the lines already, and walked toward the stage. As she reached the stairs the man who'd just been Oberon was coming down. Ava looked at him and stumbled on the first step, landing painfully on her knee. The man reached down to help her and Ava looked up into his eyes, which, she couldn't help noticing, were the warm brown of hot cocoa, and managed to say thank you. But her knee was throbbing so badly she had to fight back tears. She limped onto center stage and tried to focus on the words she knew so well.

But suddenly, they were gone. In their place was a vision of warm brown eyes and a feeling of panic. She looked down and noticed that she was still holding the script. Thank God! She turned quickly to the page where Titania enters the stage and began. The words felt like lead in her mouth. The airy grace and strong passion which she usually had at her command verbally were somehow hobbled. Ava began to sweat and she could hear a sickening tremble in her voice. After the longest ninety seconds of her life she finished reading the speech, and there was a pattering of polite applause.

"Thank you Ava," said Troy. Then he stood up and said, "I want to thank you all for coming. I will post the cast tomorrow in the theatre lobby. I hope those of you who don't get a part this time will consider helping out backstage. Again, thank you all for coming."

And that was it. He started gathering up his things and when he stood up Ava could see he was half a foot shorter than she was, which made her even angrier. For, now that she had hobbled back to her seat and sat down, Ava knew without being told that there was no way in hell she was going to get the part of Titania. And if the director asked her to play Helena, well . . . She shook her head dismally. Maybe her mother was right.

Ava buttoned up her coat and started walking up the aisle, concentrating on her feet and relieved that the pain in her knee was subsiding at least. When she got to the door Troy was there, holding it open for her. She looked down at his face and he smiled warmly.

"Hey, I hope you'll consider the part of Helena, Ava. I know it's not the one you wanted, but you're really perfect for the role."

Ava smiled grimly. "Yes. I know," she said, and limped away.

Troy looked after her with a puzzled expression. She really was attractive in an offbeat sort of way. *And she's really tall*, he noted with approval, adding to the list of her charms.

Ever since he was a young boy looking up to his sister, Troy had admired women who stood above the rest. It wasn't until he was enrolled in dance class in sixth grade that he discovered the admiration wasn't reciprocated by the taller girls who declined to dance with him because of his lack of inches. When he gained some stature as a teenager, Troy continued to be intrigued by taller girls, but no matter how he tried, they seemed immune to his appeals.

When Troy had discussed the problem with his sister, she had explained to him that most girls are brainwashed from infancy to believe that men should be taller than women. From Prince Charming to Prince William, the unwritten rules were clear, and after a few years of experiencing rejections from willowy leggy girls, Troy reluctantly accepted that his sister knew what she was talking about.

But, that didn't mean he agreed with it.

Chapter Two

It was nearly 10:00 by the time Ava turned the key in her apartment door, but she could hear her phone ringing from the hall and she had a pretty good idea who it would be.

"Hello?"

"So, how'd it go? Did you slay them with your awesome fairy queenness?"

Ava slumped onto her couch with her coat still on. "I don't think I actually slayed anyone, but I definitely did some damage to my knee."

"What happened?"

Ava felt a little better once she'd told Chenille all about slipping on her way to the stage and then panicking and pretty much blowing the audition. But, she could feel tears of disappointment crowding behind her eyes and she almost wished Chenille wouldn't be so darn cheerful. It kind of made it worse.

"Well, so it sounds like he wants you for Helena? That's good isn't it? I mean, a part's a part. A rose by any other name . . ."

"Stinks. Helena is the buffoon of the play."

"That's not true, Ava. Aren't you forgetting that whole bit with Bottom and the donkey head and all those jokes about being an ass? I mean, come on, Helena winds up with a handsome guy at the end. That's romance. You could have a lot of fun."

Ava frowned, but she knew Chenille was right. If she got the part of Helena, it would be a good start. After all, it was an important role. She sighed. "You're right. I'm sure I'll learn a lot and it'll probably be fun."

"Oh boy, I can't wait. I'll assign my class to go see it and we'll cheer for you."

Ava smiled. Chenille might be deluded when it came to her romantic viewpoint, but she never failed to make Ava feel better. Chenille firmly believed that anyone could live happily ever after, for real, if they set their minds to it. She was incredibly adept at avoiding reality and utterly shameless when it came to romance. She was always scaring men off with her intensity. She could recite Shelley at twenty paces. She had commitment written all over her and in her game plan there was no such thing as a one night stand. More a one life stand.

So far Chenille hadn't found a man willing to get with the program, but she was supremely confident that her Mr. Perfect would arrive in her life at exactly the right time. Ava figured that's why Chenille managed to be so cheerful all the time. Unlike Ava, who wasn't even sure that a Mr. Perfect existed, much less that he'd show up in her life.

After she hung up the phone, though, the image of that hunky Oberon character rose in her mind and just thinking about him made her feel overheated. Then she noticed that she still had her coat on and laughed at herself. *Slow down, Ave,* she told herself. *You're not in that guy's league.*

But, she mused, another reason to accept the part of Helena would be that it would guarantee seeing more of that delicious Oberon. Ooh, yeah. No harm in looking, she thought.

Troy arrived late to his office the next morning, having stopped by the theatre to post the cast list. He checked his answering machine and decided to let Mrs. Trevor wait while he returned Nina's call.

"Nina? Hi, yeah. We've got a cast." Troy held the receiver a few inches from his ear anticipating the response from his producer, who, though she'd retired from the stage, still had the ability to make her lines heard all the way in the back row.

"So? Tell me. Who showed up? Did we get a good Oberon? Please tell me you did not have to give Winston Ferris the part." In her long and tempestuous involvement in the local community theater scene Nina Hendrix had gotten to know all the usual players. She had her favorites and, though she was kind to the less than talented, she had the ruthless drive for perfection that made her either a valuable ally or a frightening foe. She was unfailingly generous with her opinions.

"You know, I don't think he even showed up. Maybe he's sick."

"That wouldn't stop Winston. Maybe he died."

Troy smiled. "Actually, we got some really good people, I think. One woman who read for Titania was exceptional. Her name is Marion Zimmer."

"Really? I saw her in *Medea* years ago, up in Alexandria. She was pretty good I thought. I'm surprised. I wonder if she's moved to Richmond. That would be great if she has."

"Yeah. So she's Titania. And Oberon was no contest either. Do you know a guy named Howard Lyon?"

"Howard!" Troy jerked the phone another foot away from his ear.

"Yeah. Tall guy, kind of good looking. He's got great stage presence."

"Tell me about it. Jeez. Howard. I remember when we did *The Importance of Being Earnest,* one of my last performances. I played his grandmother. Howard was just starting out, and he was quite the hottie back then. I'll bet he's still got it." Nina paused. "Kind of full of himself, though, as I recall."

"Well, he seemed nice enough last night. And he certainly looks the part."

"How about the rest?"

"I think we're in good shape. A bunch of students showed up and a couple of them are good enough for Demetrius and Lysander. And the girl for Hermia is fine." Troy paused, remembering how disappointed Ava was going to be to learn that she was to be Helena.

"Well that's great then. And you got a Helena."

Troy hesitated. "Yeah. She's a little older than our Hermia, but I think she'll do. I mean, she looks the part."

"Tall?"

"She's almost too tall. Luckily the kid playing Demetrius is built like a center forward."

"That would be a basketball term?"

"Right. The thing is, she doesn't want to be Helena, and I can't blame her. It's an awkward part, and this woman looked uncomfortable on stage already."

"Does she have any experience?"

"No. But she seems intelligent. I'm just hoping she can take direction."

"Well, you ought to tell her she's lucky to get to play Helena. It's the best part."

"Oh come on. I've seen the play dozens of times. Helena is the Carol Burnett of the show."

"Listen pal, Carol Burnett was no fool. And I think you're missing something. Think about it. Who really cares about Titania and Oberon and their little custody battle? Who cares about Pyramus and Thisbe, for God's sake? And Hermia's a spoiled prima donna who isn't even loyal to her so-called best friend. So you've got this love quadrangle with girl loves boy who loves another girl who loves another boy. And the only one nobody loves, at the start, is Helena. The audience should be rooting for her, but they don't because most directors don't get it. She gets more action than anyone else in the play, and she's the most honestly passionate character. It's a great role. That's what you've got to make this girl understand."

"She's not a girl."

"Okay, woman." Nina paused. "You don't sound convinced."

"I'm thinking. I have to admit I never thought about Helena like that. You know, usually there's this Tweedledum, Tweedledee thing with the young lovers."

"I know. But I'm telling you, Helena's the salt that makes the stew tasty. Without her it would be near beer."

"What?"

"Alcohol-free beer. Before your time I guess."

"I guess. Well, I'll think it over. Maybe I'll talk to Ava."

"That's Helena?"

"Yeah."

"Good theatre name, Ava. Who've you got for Bottom, by the way?"

"Oh, it was just as you predicted."

"Tim Murphy?"

"You called it."

"Hah. Well, at least he knows how to do comedy. I just don't approve when he tries to play King Lear or something."

"So, we're all set, I think. Rehearsals start tomorrow night. You coming?"

"I'll give you a day or two to toughen them up. I've got a lot going on this week. Look for me on Thursday."

"Okay. See you then."

Troy hung up feeling grateful that he'd persuaded Nina to take on the thankless task of producer—all the headaches and none of the glory. Luckily, she'd had her share of applause already, and now it seemed she enjoyed the subtler pleasures to be found backstage.

Thinking of that world, the behind the curtain excitement of makeup, costumes, and wordplay, Troy couldn't help smiling. It was really happening. His first production. He looked at the graph paper on his table, knowing that he should get back to Mrs. Trevor's koi problem, but all he wanted to do was sketch set designs. He hoped enough of the students who showed up last night would be willing to help out building the sets. He certainly couldn't afford to pay anyone. The theatre group just barely managed to pay rent on the building, and it wasn't in such great shape either.

Troy shrugged off these concerns. This morning, at least, he would allow himself the luxury of feeling happy and optimistic. His first production. He would make it a success. He would do whatever had to be done.

The following night Ava was so nervous about the first rehearsal that she decided to walk to the theatre to burn off her excess anxiety. Of course, if she had found her spare car keys by now she probably would have driven, but she hadn't had the time or energy to look for them yet. She was convinced they'd turn up, if she pretended she didn't care.

Before leaving her apartment, she gave herself a little lecture in the mirror.

"I am a deeply fascinating babe in need of nothing and no one." It was a mantra she'd read once in a magazine article about self-esteem, and, though she scoffed at pop psychology, the phrase had resonated somehow with her, and she used it on herself whenever her confidence needed a jump-start.

Tonight, she'd do better than she had at that awful audition. She just had to relax. She stepped out onto Monument Avenue and began striding swiftly toward the theatre, just twelve blocks away. It was a nice evening. Chilly, but not unpleasantly so, and light still lingered in the air although it was almost 7:00. After she had walked three blocks she noticed a trio of students just ahead of her and guessed that they might be headed for the same destination. Ava slowed her pace, not eager to catch up to them. She hadn't recognized any of her own students at the auditions, and, it was possible these students weren't heading for the theatre, but as she gained on them she thought she could hear the words Puck and Lysander. Ava stopped walking and waited till the students got a whole block ahead.

What's wrong with you Ava? You're going to have to work

with these kids, she thought. She wondered if any of them had seen her sorry attempt at Titania. She shook her head. *Get a grip Ave. They don't care. They're kids. They're not trying to prove anything.* Ava watched the students for a moment, the way they laughed with each other, the skip in their steps. She sighed and dug her hands in her pockets and started walking slower. *When did I get so old?* she thought.

By the time she reached the theatre Ava had determined not to be intimidated by anyone. Not even that Titania. When she stepped in the first person she saw was the hunk playing Oberon and he looked over and met her eyes and Ava's veneer of cool shattered. God, the guy was hot looking.

"Ava! I'm glad you could come."

She looked around and saw the director smiling up at her. What was his name? She frowned slightly. "Did you think I wouldn't?" she asked.

"No. No. It's just, I know you have a job and I didn't know if you'd be able to come," said Troy, smiling in a friendly way that irritated Ava for no good reason.

"I'm sorry," she said. "I don't think I caught your name."

"Troy. Troy Burnett. Please call me Troy."

Ava looked at Troy's hazel eyes, his light brown hair. "Okay. Troy." She smiled slightly, since he seemed to be expecting some kind of response. But really, she thought, *Troy?* She went in to the theatre and sat down near a group of students who were chattering noisily. They all seemed to know each other. Ava looked around and noticed the woman who got Titania sitting by herself, knitting. Oberon joined the students and they welcomed him like he was one of them, with high fives and jokes.

After a few minutes Troy stepped up on the stage and told everyone that tonight would be a simple first read through. "After tonight I'll put up a schedule of rehearsals broken up by scenes, so you all won't have to be here every night until we get farther along. By the time we get to April, everyone will have to come to every rehearsal, and I also expect everyone to know all their lines by heart."

The cast assembled on stage, most sitting down on the floor, though a few of the older actors dragged folding chairs over.

"Okay," said Troy. "For the purposes of this reading, I'd like you to sort of group yourselves with your unit. That would be, Oberon and Titania with Puck and the fairies, the young lovers with the king and his court, and the rude mechanicals together. As you all probably know, *Midsummer Night's Dream* has three plot lines that weave together, plus the play within a play which the mechanicals perform. It helps to keep that structure in mind if you find yourself getting confused."

One of the older actors raised his hand.

"Yes, Marshall?"

"Do you know if you're planning to stage it as a period piece?"

"That's a good question. I know all of you have probably seen this play performed in a lot of different ways, but we're going to do it straight. I mean, we're going to keep it in Shakespeare's imaginary forest, and costumes will reflect the classic tradition—think ancient Rome or Greece."

A couple of the boys in the rude mechanical group started chanting "Toga, toga, toga."

Troy smiled indulgently. "Right. Time for that later at the cast party. Now let's begin."

Ava sat uncomfortably on the floor and listened to the slow and not particularly enthralling beginning of the play. She'd forgotten the confusing, and, it seemed to her now, completely unnecessary subplot of the King and his conquered bride. The pace picked up slightly once the girl who played Hermia stood up and began reading. Ava could hear some emotion at least. But, she thought, the guy playing Demetrius was as wooden as a tree. And tall enough too, she noticed. *He probably got the part for the same reason I did* she thought bitterly. *We'll make such a nice couple.*

After a few more minutes, during which her foot went to

sleep, the reading came to Ava's entrance and she felt the urge to stand up, but decided against it.

" 'Call you me fair? That fair again unsay,' " she read, her voice clear and, she thought, musical, compared to some of the dull voices before. Troy looked over and said, "Could you stand up when you read, Ava?"

She started to stand up, forgetting that her foot had gone to sleep, and promptly lurched forward on top of the boy who was playing Lysander. Everyone laughed and Ava felt her face turning scarlet.

"That's great stuff Ava, but save it for the show," said Troy.

She shot him a sour look and got to her feet, leaning one hand on Lysander's shoulder. "Sorry," she muttered.

She focused on her script and read her lines. The scene moved along. Ava stood there feeling nothing. Absolutely nothing. Well, not absolutely. She was beginning to actively dislike Troy. The little dweeb. At least when her Demetrius stood up and spoke his lines near her she felt some sense of scale. But, as the evening wore on Ava felt a fog of disappointment settling in her soul. Everyone else seemed to be enjoying themselves. Why couldn't she? It was especially hard when the fairies took over the stage, and Oberon and Titania declaimed their poetic lines. *Really*, thought Ava, *Shakespeare gave all the best lines to the fairies.*

The fairies in the cast certainly seemed to be having the most fun. Three girls and four boys, all of them slight of build and cute of face, were cast as the magical entourage. Noting her dyed black hair, raccoon eyeliner, and pierced nose, Ava guessed one of the girls must be planning to be the token Goth fairy. Her gaze drifted over to Oberon, whom she couldn't think of as a Howard, or worse, as Howie, as she'd heard one of the girls call him. Ava noticed he was watching Hermia flouncing as she chirped her lines. With chilling clarity Ava recognized the light in Howie's eyes. It was pure lust. Or wasn't that an oxymoron? Okay, call it impure lust, and make that Howard as a moron. Ava sighed.

Why had she thought theatre life would be any better than real life?

"Ava? That's your cue."

Ava looked up and realized she'd lost track of what scene they were doing. Troy was looking at her expectantly. Not unkindly, just patiently, like a parent. But for some reason that only made Ava more resentful. She paged quickly through the script and found her place. " 'You draw me, you hardhearted adamant!' "

"That's right," interrupted Troy, "but when we do this scene I'd like you and Demetrius to really let it rip. This is the big scene for Helena, when she bares her soul and he walks all over it. So keep that in mind when you're learning your lines. I want you two to set the stage on fire in this scene."

Three of the fairies spontaneously held up lighters, as if they were at a rock concert, and everyone laughed but Troy, who only smiled and said, "I'm serious. We'll have plenty of slapstick in this play, but I also want to keep the romance hot."

Ava looked at Demetrius, who was smirking at Lysander. She felt like slapping him. Or slapping Troy. Or, better yet, both of them. But, she clenched her fists and told herself to stay calm. Be professional now. Get revenge later.

"Okay, Troy," she said sweetly.

Later that night, when the cast was drifting out the door Ava stepped out onto the sidewalk and promptly wished she hadn't walked to the theatre. She put her head down and wrapped her coat tighter around herself and started into the cold dark.

"Hey, do you need a ride Ava?"

She looked behind her. Troy stood under the marquee.

"I'm parked right across the street."

"I just live down the street," she said.

"Okay. It's just kind of late, and cold," he said.

Ava sucked in another chilly breath and decided she could put up with him for a few blocks. "Sure. Thanks."

He led the way to a big black Ford with oversized tires. Ava noticed a graphic on the door as she climbed in. Blue Rose Landscaping.

She glanced over at Troy as he started up the truck.

"You're a landscaper?"

"That's right."

"There's no such thing as a blue rose, though, is there?"

Troy smiled at her. "That's true. Though lots of breeders are trying."

"So why name the business after something that doesn't exist?"

"Lots of things don't exist, except as ideas. That doesn't mean the ideas aren't worth considering. In our business we try to work with people's ideas, their dreams of back-yard paradise, even if they seem impossible. Like a blue rose."

"But you can't deliver a blue rose."

"No. And we never promise what we can't deliver." Troy looked at Ava, noticing how her hair brushed the ceiling of the cab of his truck. She really was tall, like a supermodel, he thought.

He turned back to watch the road. Ava glanced at the light from the streetlights casting shadows on his face. It was not a bad face, she decided.

When a red light stopped them Troy looked over at her and said, "Listen Ava, I know you didn't want the part of Helena, and I appreciate you being willing to take it on anyway. But, I really think it could be a great part for you."

Ava flinched at the condescending tone of his voice.

Troy went on. "Really, Helena is a great role. We can get a lot of laughs with visual comedy, but she's also a sympathetic character. The audience cares about her."

Ava laughed. "She's a pathetic character. Everyone mocks her. Everyone roots for Hermia, the pretty one." She paused. "This is my block. You can let me out here," she said.

Troy stopped the truck and frowned. Turning to Ava he

said, "You're wrong. Both the girls are pretty. Both of them are desirable. The only difference between them is that one is a little taller than the other. Shakespeare wrote the play to show how crazy love is, how nothing about love makes sense."

Ava's eyes widened and she looked at Troy mildly. He seemed almost upset.

"Well," she said, in a quieter voice, "it's not the part I wanted. That's true. But I do appreciate you giving me a chance. And I promise I'll do my best."

"That's all I ask. See you tomorrow," said Troy.

Ava hopped out and shut the door. She climbed the stairs and put her key in the door. She looked back and noticed Troy was waiting to make sure she got in. She gave him a little wave and went inside. She went down the hall to her apartment door and let herself in and saw the foot-high stack of papers that she had to get through before class tomorrow at 11:00. She went in the kitchen and put on some water for coffee. With any luck she could be done by 1 A.M. Through the wall of her living room she could hear the stereo in the next apartment blasting some kind of rap or hip hop.

She wondered idly if Shakespeare were alive today, would he be writing hip hop? Or would Snoop Dogg be quoted by future generations?

Humming, she sharpened her red pencil and began grading papers.

As he drove away from her, Troy gritted his teeth. He'd seen the look in Ava's eyes as she clambered out of his truck. That eagerness to get away. There wasn't even the slightest spark of interest in him as a man. *Of course, she probably thinks I'm too short to qualify,* he thought irritably as he drove around the circle beneath the statue of General Jeb Stuart. *Fine. She may be a teacher, but maybe she can still learn a few things.*

Chapter Three

The next morning when Ava checked her box at work there was a note from Chenille asking if she'd like to meet for lunch. Ava had been hoping to use the time to start memorizing her lines, but then she had the happy idea of asking Chenille to help her, so she left a message on Chenille's voice mail.

By 1:00 they had ordered their sandwiches and taken a corner table at the Wicked Redhead Café when Ava got out her script and said, "I copied the pages I need to learn so you can read them with me."

Chenille beamed. "Cool. I've always loved those scenes with the catfights."

"Huh. I thought only guys got off on watching girls fight."

"Nope. It reminds me of me and my sisters. Except of course we won't be doing any scratching or slapping."

"I wouldn't count on that," said Ava, pulling on her bangs.

"You should be glad your hair's short, at least. She'll have a hard time getting a grip on it."

Ava grinned. "I guess I should be glad I'm bigger than she is too. This director sounds like he wants us to play up the slapstick. It could get ugly."

Chenille shrugged. "Oh I don't know. It could be very therapeutic. Seems to me you've got to have a lot of untapped rage in there. You just have to be careful you don't actually injure somebody."

Ava laughed. "That could happen," she admitted.

They read through the scene a few times, finished their coffee and headed back to the school. On the way Chenille asked, "So this weekend I was thinking of going to the Maymont Flower Show. Want to come?"

Ava thought for a minute. The park at Maymont was one of the best things about living in Richmond. In addition to its acres of gardens open to the public and its historic house, Maymont offered a wealth of nature and recreational programs all year round. The winter flower show at the Richmond Convention Center helped support all that good stuff, but Ava also remembered the last time she accompanied Chenille to one of these indoor garden things, and how stupefyingly bored she'd been shuffling past the artificially arranged displays. What she really wanted to do this weekend was get outside and run. She needed to start training for the marathon in November if she was going to do it again this year. And she really wanted to do it.

"Well, I don't know. It was so crowded last year," she began.

"Yeah. But this year they've made it three days instead of two, so it won't be as bad," said Chenille, enthusiastically. "Come on. It'll be fun. I'll buy you hyacinths."

Ava smiled. She adored the fragrance of hyacinths. And, seeing the eager look in Chenille's eyes, Ava relented and agreed to go Saturday. She could run at least eight miles Sunday anyway.

Looking out the window at the gray rain Saturday morning, Ava was glad she had agreed to go to the flower show after all. Running in the rain was never fun, and cold rain was the worst. Besides, at least at the flower show she might be able to break the tape loop of Shakespearean dialogue that kept playing in her head. At rehearsal Thursday night Troy had made them run through the opening scenes so many times that Ava felt as if she could recite the entire first act. And it wasn't very entertaining.

She put on her favorite pair of jeans, a deep fuchsia turtleneck sweater that always made her feel good, and her black Nikes, knowing there would be a lot of walking, even if it was indoors. In honor of the flower show, she changed her usual sapphire studs for a pair of faux plumeria earrings, a little gaudy perhaps, but Ava thought Chenille would appreciate the touch.

And she did. "Wow, cool earrings," said Chenille, as soon as Ava slid into the car.

Ava smiled. "Thanks. My mom got them for me in Hawaii. I don't wear them very often, but I figured to-day . . ."

"Right. Good call," said Chenille. She was dressed in a long flowered skirt topped with a bright coral sweater, cut kind of low.

"You look great," said Ava.

"Thanks. I'm kind of hoping we run into this guy I told to come."

"Who?"

"I don't think you know him. He coaches the wrestling squad?"

Ava looked skeptical. "I don't have any idea who that is, but I wouldn't have thought a wrestling coach would be interested in a flower show."

"What? Can't a wrestler enjoy flowers? Haven't you seen those FTD ads with the football players? Lots of men like to grow flowers."

"I'm glad to hear it." Ava grinned. "I'm just saying, I don't think a flower show is the most likely place to pick up guys."

"Huh. We'll see about that," said Chenille.

They parked in a lot two blocks from the Convention Center and hurried through the rain to the entrance. Though it was only a little after 10A.M. the place already looked packed. Ava and Chenille got their tickets stamped and edged into the crowd. While Chenille spent a few minutes studying the floor map to determine their course, Ava peered around the vast room.

"You know, I think we might be the youngest women in the room," she said.

Chenille looked up. A woman with a fully loaded twin-seater stroller struggled past, trailing balloons and animal crackers.

"It's just your imagination. Things could be worse," Chenille said. "Come on, this way. I smell hyacinths."

Ava smiled and followed. They ambled past displays of or-chids, bonsai, tulips and topiary. They wandered through ex-hibits of complete herb gardens, rock gardens, and Japanese style contemplation gardens. After an hour Chenille spotted a bench near a display of tropical flowers and suggested they take a breather. Ava wasn't tired, but she guessed that Che-nille's stylish pumps weren't as forgiving as her Nikes.

"So, no sign of your wrestler, eh?" said Ava.

"It's early yet," said Chenille, hopefully watching the steady stream of little old ladies carrying big canvas bags. "No rehearsals for you this weekend?"

"Nope. Thank God. The director is a slavedriver, but he said we wouldn't start weekend rehearsals until April."

"What's he like, anyway? Aside from being a slavedriver?"

Ava considered the question for a moment. "He's nice."

Chenille frowned at her. "Nice? Is that it? Would you care to amplify that remark, Ms. Morrison?"

Ava shrugged. "I don't know what to say. He seems nice. He's very encouraging and patient and he has a kind of sense of humor." She frowned. "I don't know. He's nothing spe-cial. He's just nice."

Chenille studied Ava's face. "You know, I think there must be something here I'm missing. Maybe I should come to one of these rehearsals and see for myself."

Ava shook her head. "It's nothing Nille. Really. The guy who's something is Howard. Or, as the fairies say, '*And Howard.*'"

"Oh really? Tell me more."

"Didn't I tell you about him? He looks like Brendan Frazier."

"*The Mummy* dude?"

"Right. Howard's kind of like that. Big and hunky, but not, um, subtle."

"In what way is he not subtle?"

Ava rolled her eyes. "In the way he stares at Hermia, for instance."

"Oh. I see. That kind of not subtle." Chenille nodded. "Let's not forget that staring at women has been the undoing of many a poor schlubb."

"True. But some men can look a woman in the eye."

"Like the director?"

Ava looked pointedly at Chenille. "He's just nice, okay? Nothing more, nothing less."

"Right," said Chenille, widening her eyes innocently. "That's all I'm saying."

"Shall we move along?" said Ava.

"That would be nice," said Chenille, smiling sweetly.

The noise level inside the center had been steadily growing since they arrived and Ava felt oddly insulated by the echoing roar, as if she and Chenille were suspended in a bubble of privacy. Then, as they rounded a turn bordered with tubs of billowy pink hydrangeas something caught her ear. A familiar voice crystallized out of the background static. Ava looked around, searching for the source, and she saw Troy standing on a raised platform in front of a vine-covered pergola.

She stared at him for a moment, struck by how nice he looked in his khaki pants and tattersal shirt, the sleeves rolled up halfway. He seemed to be giving a talk about some gardening topic. *Well he would, wouldn't he?* she thought, suddenly realizing she should have known he would likely be there. After all, gardening was his business.

"Ava? Let's head for that water garden display." Chenille came up beside her. Ava hesitated, unsure whether she wanted to say hello to Troy or not.

Chenille looked at her quizzically. Then, following Ava's gaze, Chenille noticed Troy.

"Are we interested in learning about pergola planting? Or pergola planters?" Chenille wiggled her eyebrows comically.

Ava turned to her and smiled. "That's my director," she whispered.

"Oh!" Chenille studied Troy for a moment. "He's cute."

Ava shrugged. "He's okay."

"Oh, that's right. You said he was 'nice' as I recall."

"Right. He's a nice man."

"Also cute."

"If you think so."

"I think so. You're obviously in denial." Chenille grinned and shook her head. "Oh Ava. Admit it. He's cute."

Ava turned away. "Didn't you want to go look at some water gardens?"

Chenille cast a glance back at Troy, who had just finished his presentation. "Don't you want to say hi?"

"No. He's busy. And I don't need a pergola."

They started to walk away, but the dense throng slowed their progress and they hadn't gotten far before Ava felt a tap on her shoulder. She almost jumped.

"Oh, I'm sorry Ava. I didn't mean to startle you, but I didn't want to yell over this crowd to get your attention." Troy stood smiling beside them. Chenille beamed at him.

"Hi Troy," said Ava. "This is my friend Chenille. She loves gardening."

"Well, you came to the right place," said Troy. "I just noticed you walking by as I finished my talk. I get a booth here every year."

"I imagine it's good for business," said Chenille.

"Yeah. Business is actually too good, but you have to keep

your name out there. It's like a wood fire. You have to keep putting wood on even after you're warm or the fire will go out." As he spoke, Ava couldn't help noticing that the way Troy was looking at her was beginning to make her feel a little warmer than she liked.

"That color looks great on you," he said.

"Thanks," she murmured. While Chenille started chatting with Troy about gardens Ava stood silently by, trying to figure out why she felt only irritation. Troy was looking at her appreciatively. Shouldn't she be glad he noticed? *No. I don't care if he's noticed. Hasn't he noticed I'm half a foot taller than he is? If I wanted a little brother he could apply for the job,* she thought. She waited impatiently for Chenille to finish making small talk.

"Well, Troy, it's been nice but we've got a lot more to see here." Ava grabbed Chenille's arm and tried to steer her away.

Troy nodded. "It was nice meeting you," he said to Chenille. "See you Monday night, Ava."

He watched them disappear in the crowd, feeling slightly unsettled. The sight of Ava in that color had touched something deep inside him. She was so strikingly beautiful. Maybe it was the way she stood out from the crowd. She was literally head and shoulders above most of them. She made Troy think of some fairytale princess, mixing with the commoners. He felt a strange pang of longing as she went out of sight.

A little woman in a floral jumper tugged at his sleeve with a question and Troy shook himself and tried to remember what he was there for.

As they walked away Chenille shook her head and looked at Ava.

"What? What?" Ava returned her gaze blankly.

"What? You're asking me what? What is the matter with you? There's a nice guy who's obviously attracted to you and you just blow him off like he was a telemarketer."

"That's not true. In the first place, he's not 'obviously attracted to me.' You're just romantically delusional. And in the second place, you're overlooking what is all too obviously wrong with him."

"What? I repeat, what?" Chenille stopped walking and stood with her hands on her hips, fixing Ava with a challenging expression like an irate Pekinese demanding attention.

Ava had to smile. "Come on, Nille. You know what. I'm not overlooking him. I'm looking over him."

Chenille frowned, a Pekinese on the verge of biting. "Oh come on yourself Ava. You aren't prejudiced against him just because he's a little shorter than you. Half the men in the world are shorter than you."

"That's right. And I want a man I can look up to. Is there anything wrong with that?"

Chenille put her hands on her hips and lowered her chin. "You know, for somebody who's as tall as you are, you certainly don't seem to have much perspective. How can you, of all people, judge a man because he's not as tall as you think he should be? And yet you find fault with men if they are intimidated by your height? I mean, double standard much?"

Ava looked chagrined. After a minute she said, "I'm sorry Nille. I know you're right. I just can't help it—you know?"

Chenille shook her head in a disappointed way, a Pekinese realizing it's not going to get taken for a run in the park.

"It saddens me to think you are so limited in your view of men." Chenille looked at Ava soberly. "You know a lot of big tall guys are total jerks, don't you? And that the measure of a really great guy has nothing to do with his shoe size, or the size of any other part of his body."

Ava groaned. "Of course, I know that. But do you blame me for wanting a taller man?"

"Yes! Yes, I do. Because I think if you have this idea in your head that the right guy has to be such and such a size, then you're no better than those guys who measure every girl by the size of her . . . you know."

A prickly silence bristled between the two women for a full minute. Then Ava sighed. "Okay. You have a point. But that doesn't mean that I have to settle for Troy Boy."

Chenille rolled her eyes. "Fine. Be sarcastic and superior if you want. All I know is, he seems like a really nice guy to me, and cute too. And that makes him a contender in my book."

"Fine. He's all yours."

Chenille smiled and shook her head, giving Ava a look. "I wish."

Later that afternoon as Troy was wrapping up his fourth and final presentation for the day he saw a cluster of green and purple balloons bobbing closer, followed closely by a dark skinned man with glistening black hair.

"Hey Dad, look what we got!" Josh interrupted Troy's program without a care, like any seven-year-old confident of his dad's approval.

The man accompanying Josh knelt beside him and whispered to him to be quiet while his father gave his talk. Troy smiled at them and finished his spiel quickly.

As the small crowd dispersed Troy hopped down and gathered Josh in his arms for a hug. "So, been having a good time?"

"Yeah. Carlos and me got ice cream and we fed the fish and we swung in the hammocks."

Troy exchanged a smile with Carlos over Josh's head. "Thanks for taking him around Carlos. He would have been really bored if he'd been stuck here all day."

Carlos nodded. "Oh, we had a good time. Only thing, there's nowhere to kick a soccer ball in this whole building. We looked for some place, maybe a hallway, but no luck."

"Did you bring a soccer ball?" asked Troy.

"Of course," said Carlos, opening the gym bag he had slung over his shoulder. "Don't leave home without it."

Josh was bouncing in place beside them, energy over-flowing.

"Are you almost done Dad? Can we go to the field?"

"Just a little bit longer. Then we can go."

Carlos took the soccer ball out of his bag and began juggling it back and forth between his feet, his knees, his shoulders. Josh watched intently. Looking at his rapt face Troy suddenly felt the need to get out of this contrived space and onto a playing field. "Okay. I guess I've done enough for today. Let's go."

"Yeah!" Josh jumped and skipped all the way to the truck where the three of them squeezed in the cab. Fifteen minutes later they arrived at the field where about a dozen men and a few high school boys were running up and down, passing and kicking soccer balls. Despite the brisk late winter temperature most of the players wore shorts, like Josh and Carlos. Troy changed into his sweat pants in the truck before joining them on the field. Troy could feel his muscles loosening, his heart expanding, as his lungs filled with cold air.

For Troy, nothing untied the knots in his soul like soccer. He loved the purity. Running, kicking, the fluid give and take of the beautiful game. He knew some people thought soccer was all about hooligans and nutty fans painting their faces and going to excesses, but for Troy, it was simple. It was a game anybody could play, no matter what their size, or age, or gender. And since Josh had joined a team, Troy rejoiced at being able to share his favorite sport with his son.

Carlos and Troy both played on the Toreadors, a team in a men's weekend league, most Sundays throughout the year, outdoors most of the time, indoors in the winter. Many of the Toreadors practiced every day after work, just getting together to kick the ball around, the way some other men gather for a beer. Which is not to say that the Toreadors didn't sometimes have a beer too. But they came for love of the game.

Today, since Josh was playing, the men went a little easier, allowing him to steal the ball occasionally, even to score once. Troy watched as Josh faked a player and dribbled around him, then delivered a nice cross to a player in front of the goal. No pro could have done it better, Troy thought proudly.

They played until it got so dark they could hardly see the ball. As they were heading back to the truck one of Troy's teammates called after him. "Hey Shakespeare, you coming tomorrow?"

Troy grinned. "Sorry. Got rehearsals."

Josh looked up at him gravely. "Gee Dad, you shouldn't miss your team practice."

Troy looked at Josh fondly. "Don't worry Josh. I'll keep my skills up. But play rehearsals are important too. They're kind of like a different team practice."

Josh frowned. "Is it as much fun as soccer?"

Troy was silent for a moment. "It's a different kind of fun." Josh looked skeptical.

"Tell you what, when we start having rehearsals on the weekends you can come and watch and you can decide for yourself."

Troy expected Josh to welcome this idea, the way he usually embraced any new adventure. But the light in Josh's eyes clouded.

"My team plays on weekends. Aren't you going to come to my games?"

Troy's face fell. "Of course I am. You know I would never miss your games." He patted Josh's leg. "But after your games, maybe you can come and see some of the play rehearsals. It's got some funny parts."

Josh looked doubtful. Troy had once taken him to see a performance of *Oliver*, thinking that it might get him interested in the theatre, but Josh had squirmed in his seat for most of the show and had nothing good to say about it afterward. Still, this would be different, Troy hoped. Josh would get to see how a show came together, how the actors joked around during rehearsals. Plus, there was a lot of funny stuff in the play.

They stopped for pizza on the way home and by the time they dropped Carlos off Josh had regained his good spirits. Troy stopped at Blockbuster to let him pick out a video game to play before bed, and when they arrived Josh eagerly turned on the machine even before his father had a chance to turn the lights on. Troy shook his head and smiled, watching Josh's face lit by the pulsing video glow. Then he noticed the red light blinking on his answering machine near the kitchen.

He punched the replay button and at the sound of his sister's voice his heart sank. He was counting on her to take Josh to a birthday party tomorrow while he did his shift at the flower show.

"Troy? It's me, Jenny. Listen, I'm really sorry to have to do this, but at the last minute Ashley got invited to play in a travel tournament in Fredericksburg tomorrow and Bill's out of town and no one else I know is going so I'm going to have to drive her up there. I'm sorry. I know I said I'd take Josh to his party. And I would have been glad to. But now I just can't. I hope you can find someone else. I'm really sorry. If you want, if you just need someone to look after Josh he could come with me and Ashley to the tournament. It might be fun. Anyway. I'm sorry. Bye."

Troy slumped onto a chair in the kitchen and sighed. He could ask Carlos to come again and baby-sit Josh, but he didn't want to impose on his friend for the whole weekend. Carlos had a life. Maybe he could bring Josh to the show and just slip out for a while to drive him to the party. And then later he'd have to drive back and . . .

Bing, zeeeeooo. The video game soundtrack crackled and popped in the living room. Troy felt guilty enough already allowing his son to zone out with video games. But, all the kids did it these days. Didn't they? Maybe he could bring a TV and set it up behind the booth, let Josh play video games at the flower show? Troy stared at the sink still full of the dirty dishes from last night and this morning's hurried breakfast. Suddenly he felt an overwhelming desire to lie down and sleep. Bang, zip, wheeeooo.

Troy got to his feet wearily and walked in and sat down behind Josh on the couch. After a few minutes he said, "Hey Josh?"

"Yeah?" Josh didn't take his eyes off the screen or his thumbs off the control panel.

"Your Aunt Jenny just called. She's not going to be able to take you to the party tomorrow."

"Okay." Troy blinked. Josh's voice didn't sound disappointed at all.

"Josh? Did you hear me? Aunt Jenny can't take you to the party tomorrow and I don't know if I . . ."

"It's okay Dad," Josh interrupted. "I don't care about the party. It's just some girl in my class. She's not like my friend."

Troy leaned back on the couch. "Are you sure?"

"Yeah. It's cool."

Troy smiled, watching Josh's quick reflexes as he maneuvered his video hero through a monster-filled labyrinth. Then he remembered what Jenny had said about the tournament. "Hey Josh, your cousin Ashley is playing in a travel tournament tomorrow in Fredericksburg. Aunt Jenny said you could come along and watch if you want. Then you wouldn't have to come hang out at the flower show with me tomorrow."

"Really?" Josh turned to his father, his face lit up. "Yeah. Can I do that? I mean, the flower show was okay, but, you know."

Troy smiled. "Yeah, I know. It's not soccer. Okay. I'll call Aunt Jenny and tell her you'd like to go."

"Great!" Josh turned back to the video screen, instantly absorbed again.

Troy could feel himself slipping toward melancholy, but

he clenched his teeth and stood up, resisting the downward pull of regret. He was a single parent. Palming his kid off on his good natured sister came with the territory. He went back in the kitchen to call her.

Chapter Four

Love looks not with the eyes, but with the mind; Act 1, Sc. 1

The click click of Marion Zimmer's knitting needles measured the minutes ticking by as Ava watched the deadly dull first moments of the play. *If I were directing this I'd toss this entire bit*, she thought to herself, watching Troy trying to resuscitate the zombie playing Theseus.

The action picked up as soon as Heather bounced on stage, whining about her boyfriend like a modern teenager. Ava had tried to have a conversation with the girl earlier, before the rehearsal got underway, and the attempt only confirmed Ava's sense of being the odd-woman-out in the production. Heather had raved about some concert she'd gone to over the weekend and how she had no time to learn her lines. Ava resisted the urge to tell her that she already knew both parts.

Finally the freeze-dried characters vacated the stage and Ava went up to join Heather, Jason, and Brad, the intrepid trio whose cell phone signature tunes were already seared on Ava's memory board.

"Okay, lovers," said Troy. "I want you to use your whole bodies when you're speaking. With Shakespearean dialogue

41

you've got to help the audience get the sense of the double entendres through body language, and subtlety won't carry past the footlights. So when in doubt, use broad strokes."

Ava heard Howard murmur just loud enough for her to catch, "Broad stroking is my favorite." She pretended not to hear.

Ava stood in the center of the stage and spoke her opening lines, concluding with,

" 'O, teach me how you look and with what art

You sway the motion of Demetrius' heart!' "

And Heather goggled at her as if she were speaking Swahili.

"I'm sorry. Is that where I start?" Heather looked out at Troy questioningly.

" 'I frown upon him . . . ' " Troy prompted. Heather gaped at Ava.

" 'I frown upon him, yet he loves me still,' " said Troy patiently.

"Oh, right. 'I frown upon him, but he still loves me,' " said Heather, smiling, her ponytail swinging with each nod of her head.

"No. It's 'yet he loves me still,' " said Troy.

"Isn't that what I said?" asked Heather.

"No. Try it again. Helena, give Hermia her cue again."

Ava repeated her last couplet and waited. Heather frowned and said, "I frown at him but, yet he loves me still."

Troy sighed. Ava looked at him. Troy looked at Heather and said, "Okay, I know you haven't had much time to learn the lines yet. Has somebody got a script Heather can use?"

With script in hand, Heather managed to get through the scene, but when she exited, Ava had the stage to herself to deliver Helena's first long speech, explaining how she plans to regain Demetrius' affection. Ava spoke the lines with passion and perfection and when she finished she felt pleased with herself.

"All right," said Troy, when she finished. "Ava, you need to do more than just say the lines. If everyone just says the lines this play won't work. Try to use your whole body as you speak, especially when you're alone on the stage. You've got to give the audience visual cues to help them understand your frustration and your desperation."

Ava pursed her lips and frowned at Troy. "So what do you want me to do? Wave my arms? Jump up and down?"

"Waving your arms might help. Maybe storming back and forth across the stage. Think Mick Jagger."

Ava scowled. "Okay. If that's what you want."

Troy smiled. "Just try to be a little more active okay?"

"Fine." Ava went back to her seat fuming. She thought she'd nailed the speech. And Troy was giving her a hard time after Heather hadn't even known her lines? Was that fair?

Ava sat back in her seat and glanced over at Marion, whose knitting needles continued without a pause. Marion met her gaze, and raised her eyebrows in a silent gesture of sympathy and Ava relaxed slightly, feeling grateful for the older woman's support. Maybe she was overreacting. After all, it was early yet. Maybe Heather would get her act together.

Ava leaned back and watched the rude mechanicals going through their first scene. The six men capered about the stage like arthritic chimpanzees, milking each line for all it was worth. They got laughs from lines that had no obvious humor in them at all, and Ava felt humbled by how well the men knew their lines and how easily they played off each other. When she found herself giggling at their antics she looked over and saw Troy nodding as he watched. *Okay, flapping and storming. Can do*, she thought.

The knitting needles stopped and Ava looked over. Marion was standing up and stretching. Howard was already on-stage, joking with Nigel Fairweather, the British theatre major who got the part of Puck. Nigel looked like Martin Short and standing next to him Howard looked even more like a god. As they began their first scene together, Ava sucked in her breath at the contrast between Puck and

Oberon. Howard stood rotating from side to side as he declaimed, while Puck darted about like a fox terrier. You wanted to throw him a stick.

Then Marion stepped out and the center of gravity seemed to shift. Even without the benefit of stage lights or costume, Marion projected magical nobility. Ava studied the way Marion used her arms and rolled her shoulders, ratcheting up the drama in her long opening speech. Her feet hardly moved but her body spoke volumes.

Ava sighed. She would so have loved to be Titania. *But*, she thought, *I could never look like that*. Ava turned to watch Troy, his face intent, his expression thoughtful. When the actors finished the scene he said, "Very nice. Fairies, I'd like to see a little more fluttering. I don't want you to upstage Titania but you should be expanding her aura of mystery."

"Ooooh. I'm an expanding aura," said the Goth fairy, whose name, Ava read from the cast list, was Iris. Iris twirled past Marion, and several other fairies followed suit.

"That's nice. We might want to work up a little dance business for you all to do," said Troy. Iris glowed at him.

Troy looked at his watch and said, "It's late. I guess that will be all for tonight. Tomorrow I'd like to see all of you here same time. Keep working on memorizing your lines. You can't really begin to act until you have the words down."

Ava gathered her things and headed up the aisle. Brad, the boy playing Demetrius, touched her elbow as she passed and said, "Hey Ava, we're going to the Tavern for a beer. Want to come?"

Ava smiled, but declined the offer. "I've got papers to grade," she said, even though it wasn't true. She was just tired, and didn't want to listen to Heather babbling about Eminem. "Thanks anyway."

Outside the theatre she noticed the fairies huddled under a streetlight. As she walked by Iris called out, "G'night Helena."

Ava smiled. "Fair thee well Peaseblossom," she replied.

The fairies smiled and bowed in response and Ava walked back to her apartment feeling oddly cheered by their

warmth. Halfway home though, she frowned in sudden recollection of her car, still sitting in the lot at the park. *This is
really stupid*, Ava thought. *I should get my car before somebody tows it away. Or vandalizes it.*

The thing was, living in the city, she seldom really needed
a car. But, still, having one meant she could go to the beach
or run up to DC if she got inspired. She promised herself she
would dig out the spare set of keys by the weekend, and go
reclaim her car.

Troy spent the next morning installing a knot garden in a
suburban backyard in Willow Oaks and the whole time he
was planting the tiny boxwoods his head was swimming
with ideas for sets for the play. He could hardly wait to do
some sketches. But, when he finally got back to the office his
answering machine was full and by the time he finished
dealing with current and future clients it was nearly 4:00.

Troy tried to remember if he'd had lunch. It seemed like
he would remember if he had. The growling of his stomach
suggested not. He was just deciding to go for an early dinner
and head over to the theatre when the phone rang again and,
seeing on the caller ID that it was Nina, he picked up.

"Hey. I thought I'd stop by if you're not too busy."

"Actually, I was just going out for a bite of dinner. I
missed lunch."

"Wow. That busy huh?"

"Yeah. It's that time of year."

"Can I meet you somewhere?"

"Okay. The Grill?"

"In half an hour?"

"I'll be there in ten minutes. I'm starving."

"Okay," said Nina. "I'll get there as quick as I can."

Troy was halfway through his bowl of chili by the time
Nina slid into the seat across from him. "Sorry," he said. "I
couldn't wait."

"I wouldn't have wanted you to," Nina said, shrugging out
of her blue wool cape. With her blunt cut silver hair, severe

profile and dark prominent eyes, Nina gave the impression of being a woman who didn't take orders from anyone. The cape was part of her trademark impresario image, since not many people outside of professional magicians wore them. Nina was a magician in her own way, in getting people to do what she wanted them to.

"So, how are things?" she began.

Troy paused for half a beat. "Well, I think we're making progress."

"And?"

"And, there's still some things that are going to take some work."

"Like what?"

Troy shrugged. "Nothing major. The mechanicals are fine. And Titania's excellent. The kids aren't learning their lines as fast as I'd like."

"Which kids?"

"Demetrius and Lysander. Brad and Jason." Troy paused. "And Heather . . ."

"Heather is Hermia?"

"Yeah. She's kind of an airhead."

"Typecasting eh?"

Troy smiled. "Maybe I'm expecting too much. It's only the first week."

Nina shook her head. "No. You need to put the pressure on them early. Because later on there'll be plenty of other things to fix. They need to get the lines cold in the first two weeks. If you don't nag them, they'll put it off. Especially the kids. They think it's like cramming for an exam."

Troy nodded.

"How about the older one, Helena?"

Troy's face became thoughtful. "Well. She knows the lines. But she's so stiff onstage. I don't know how to loosen her up. Every time I make a suggestion she freezes even more."

"Hmmm. Maybe she needs to hear it from someone else."

"But I'm the director. She should be listening to me, no?"

"Yes and no. Sometimes these amateurs get mule-ish. The harder you push 'em the more they dig in. Maybe if you just leave her alone she'll come around."

Troy looked doubtful. "Maybe. You coming tonight?"

"Thought I might, yeah."

"Good. You can see what I mean. Maybe you can think of something."

"Okay."

Two hours later in the dark theatre Nina leaned over to Troy and whispered, "Gosh. You weren't kidding."

On stage Ava was rehearsing her first scene with Demetrius, and Nina cringed as she listened to Ava's melo-dramatic reciting. After Brad's line, "Tempt not too much the hatred of my spirit, For I am sick when I do look on thee," Ava said, " 'And I am sick when I look not on you.' "

"Boy, I'm going to be sick if she doesn't lighten up," whispered Nina.

Troy shook his head and whispered back. "Yeah. That's what I meant."

"Does she know this is a comedy?" asked Nina.

"I think she's trying," said Troy.

Nina listened as Ava finished the scene, missing not one word, but missing every chance to get a laugh.

"Sheesh," said Nina, when it was over. "I'd hate to see that girl do tragedy. Although, maybe she'd mess that up too. People will laugh if you try to be too serious."

Troy frowned. "I don't know what to say to her."

Nina shook her head. "It's tricky."

Ava came down off the stage and smiled at Troy, serenely confident that she had made no mistakes in the scene. Mean-while Howard and Nigel carried on in the important scene where Oberon decides to micromanage the quarreling lovers.

"Where did this Puck come from?" whispered Nina.

"I think he's some kind of exchange student," whispered Troy.

"He's got the right build for the part," said Nina.

"Yeah. And he's done Shakespeare before. He knows how to work the lines."

"Maybe he could coach Helena?"

Troy looked skeptical. "I don't know. She's kind of serious, I think. And he's kind of . . ."

"Not?"

"Right."

"That could be just what the doctor ordered."

"Maybe."

"Why don't you tell him to coach Helena a bit. Seeing as how he's British and all, maybe she'd be receptive."

Troy watched in silence for a moment. "Okay," he said finally. "I'll have a word with Nigel."

At the end of the night Troy took Nigel aside, after first making sure Ava had left the building.

"Nigel, I wonder if you could give Ava a few pointers on how to move on stage?"

"Do you think she'd like that?" Nigel's acidic English accent gave his every utterance a skeptical twist.

"Well, I don't know if she'd like it. But she needs help loosening up on stage, and I was thinking, since you understand Shakespeare, maybe she'd be more willing to listen to you. She doesn't seem to respond to my suggestions."

A crooked smile twisted Nigel's small face. "I see." He was silent for a minute, weighing the idea. Then his expression shifted and he said, "Sure. I'll have a word with her. Jolly her along. Anything to help the show, right?"

"Thanks. I appreciate it."

Nigel nodded complacently. "Yeah. It's a fact, isn't it? You yanks love the Bard, but he's a bit much for most American actors. I'm not surprised our Ava is having a tough go. She's got the words all right, but she doesn't act like she knows what they mean."

Troy's eyes darkened. "Well, I know she wants to do a good job. She might be trying too hard. Maybe you can just help her to relax a little bit."

Troy thought he saw an impish gleam flicker in Nigel's face for a second, but then Nigel looked at him seriously and nodded. "I'll take care of it."

Troy watched him walk away, feeling uneasy despite Nigel's blithe assurance. But, a few minutes later he shook himself and decided it couldn't hurt to have Nigel give Ava a few pointers.

The next night at rehearsals Troy noticed Nigel chatting with Ava before they got to work. Nigel was gesturing broadly and grinning. He seemed to be doing all of the talking. Ava was standing there listening, her arms folded, her face a mask of tolerance. Seeing her at this distance Troy suddenly flashed on a memory of his mother, listening patiently to one of his overambitious ideas. That's what Ava reminded him of—a mother putting up with a child's silliness.

When Nigel finally paused and smiled at Ava, clearly expecting her approval, Ava smiled, a quiet Mona Lisa smile Troy thought, and said something Troy couldn't hear. Her body language was clear enough, though. And later on, when they got to the scenes with Helena, Ava seemed almost more rigid than before. Troy tried to suppress the irritation swelling inside him. Ava seemed intelligent. More than that. She seemed sensitive and aware. Why couldn't she understand what the role of Helena required?

"Don't worry, boss. She's a stubborn one, our Ava. But I've got a plan."

Nigel had slithered next to Troy and whispered at his ear. "What plan?"

"Plan B," whispered Nigel, touching his nose with his index finger and waggling his eyebrows conspiratorially. "Don't worry. You'll see. Have her right as rain tomorrow."

Troy frowned. "Maybe you should leave her alone."

Nigel looked surprised. "No. Trust me. Plan B. Can't miss. You'll see."

Troy stared at the stage, where Ava looked like a teacher monitoring recess, her expression a blend of boredom and frustration. Against his will Troy began to feel angry. He'd given her a good part, and this was how she acted. Acted! That was the problem. She couldn't act. She was great at reciting, but she couldn't for one minute forget her own self. Before he knew he was going to do it Troy stood up and said loudly, "Stop!"

Brad, Jason, and Heather stopped moving and Ava looked blandly out at Troy. Her composure infuriated him.

"Can anyone tell me what is wrong with this scene?" he asked, addressing the rest of the actors waiting in their seats.

No one said anything.

Troy glared up at the stage. "Helena, Hermia has just threatened to scratch your eyes out. Lysander has just told you he loves you. Demetrius has said he loves you more. Why are you just standing there? Are you breathing? Is your heart beating? I ask because it's not obvious from here."

Ava's eyes widened and she stared at Troy as if he were a poisonous snake. Her cheeks felt hot and if she weren't so mad she knew she would probably cry, but luckily, she was furious.

"I'm 'standing here' waiting for someone else to say their line properly. Perhaps you haven't noticed, but none of these three has managed to say one of their lines without forgetting a word or a whole phrase. I don't see how my bouncing around like a two year old is going to help." Ava glared at Troy in the silence that followed.

Troy looked at the floor for a moment, his lips set in a tight line. Then he met Ava's angry eyes and said, "I'm not saying you don't have a point, Ava. I have already spoken to the rest of the cast about the importance of learning their lines. And I appreciate that you are one of the few who made the effort. But, that doesn't alter the fact that you need to move on the stage. You can't stand there like a stone while all the other actors are in motion. That's not Helena's character. She's a drama queen. She takes chances. She's aggressive and passionate and you've got to show that with your body."

A wolf whistle from someone in the audience broke the tension. Ava avoided looking at Brad and Jason and Heather. Troy sighed and said, "All right. Let's move to a different scene for now. Oberon? Let's have you and Puck in Act Three, Scene Two." Troy sat down and for the rest of the night he concentrated on not meeting Ava's eyes, but he could feel her anger scorching him from across the auditorium. In the back of his mind he felt the urge to have it out with her, to tell her that he expected more from her because he could sense it was there. He could feel the passion banked behind her stony gaze and it moved him in ways that made him uncomfortably aware of how long it had been since he'd held a woman in his arms. He tried not to look at her to suppress the emotions she roused in him.

Plus, if he was honest with himself, he knew that at some level he was beginning to feel frustrated by Ava's remoteness. She didn't chat with the rest of the cast, she didn't open up to anyone. It wasn't just him. Although, Troy suspected that if only she'd confide in him he wouldn't care if she said a word to anyone else.

When the actors were filing out of the theatre after 10:00, Troy nudged Nigel as he passed and said, "Plan B?"

Nigel winked. "Plan B."

Chapter Five

When Chenille stopped into Ava's office the following afternoon she found her drumming her fingers on the windowsill and staring moodily out the window.

"Hey, how goes the show?"

"Hmmph. Depends on who you ask."

"I asked you."

"Okay. For me, it's going just great. Really great. The director thinks I have all the acting talent of a tombstone and half the cast haven't bothered to take the time from their busy lives to learn their lines, and, oh, did I mention that now I'm getting extra special coaching from the little dweeb who thinks he's God's gift to us Americans who have no clue when it comes to Shakespeare? So, yeah. It's going great."

Chenille pulled a chair next to Ava and donned her best 'I-feel-your-pain' expression. "Not going so good huh? What's the problem?"

Ava sighed and opened the window, leaning her forearms on the sill, resting her chin on her hands. The new spring sun felt good on her pale skin and she longed for a moment to just forget the whole thing—the play, her job, her lonely existence—and disappear onto some tropical island, where, even if her personal problems followed her, they would have a hard time making such pests of themselves in the palm tree and margarita-rich environment.

"I don't know. Everything's okay, I guess." She tilted her head to one side and looked at Chenille, a poster girl for spring's eternal hope dressed in lavender and lace.

Ava sat up. "Last night Nigel gave me a lecture."

"Who's Nigel?"

"He's the English guy. He plays Puck. And, I guess being English makes him our on-site Shakespearean expert, because last night he told me what I was doing wrong."

"Was it good advice?"

Ava frowned. "I don't know. It's the same crap the director has been telling me so I don't know if that means it's good advice or that they both hate me."

"But we're not paranoid, right? Just because they're out to get us."

Ava smiled. "Right." She shook her head. "I don't know Nille. Maybe I am too stiff on stage. I know my lines, but I don't know what to do with my hands. Or my feet. Or my face. A lot of the time."

Chenille's forehead puckered with concern. "Well, you haven't done this before right? You must have known there would be some rough parts. But, this is what you've always wanted to do, right? You shouldn't get so discouraged. You'll get the hang of it. It's only, what? The second week? Once you relax I just know you're gonna be great."

Ava reached for Chenille's hand. "Thanks Nille. I've just got to learn to take criticism. Even if that little dweeb annoys the hell out of me."

"And which little dweeb are we talking about here? The Brit or the director?"

"The Brit. And the director. In that order." Ava grinned. "Thanks for listening."

"My pleasure. Maybe I should come to one of your rehearsals. Maybe I could help you tweak your role?"

Ava brightened. "That might be nice. You might get bored fast though. There's so much repetition and sitting around waiting."

"I'll be the judge of that. I can always bring along a stack of papers to grade. I'll see if I can get there tonight."

"Okay. You could at least get to check out Howard."

"The hottie?"

"In tights, too."

"Wow. Save me seat."

That night after throwing her book bag onto a seat in the theatre and getting Chenille settled Ava caught a delicious coffee aroma. She turned and saw Nigel bearing down on her with a bright smile and a paper cup.

"I heard you were a coffee lover, Ava, so I brought you this. It's a Moonlight Latte, a specialty at my favorite café."

Ava's distaste for Nigel softened as she inhaled the magic bean fragrance. Accepting the cup, which had a design of silver moons and stars on a deep blue background, she smiled and said, "It's so pretty. And it smells wonderful. Thank you Nigel. I *do* love coffee. That was very thoughtful of you."

Nigel shrugged. "I thought it was the least I could do. I hope I didn't offend you yesterday, trying to give you advice. I just want you to know I think you're going to be great as Helena."

Nigel finished up with a winsome smile and for half a second a spur of doubt jangled in Ava's inner ear, but then she breathed in another dose of intoxicating steam from the cup in her hands and decided she shouldn't be so cynical. Maybe Nigel really was just trying to be friendly. She smiled at him and said, "Thanks Nigel. I really appreciate your support."

Nigel just nodded and walked away and Ava took a sip from the cup. *Wow!* she thought. *This is really incredibly good.* The steamy sweet brew warmed her chest as it went down and Ava felt a comforting glow soothing her nerves. She sat down, sipping the coffee slowly, and looked around the theatre.

Troy was in his usual spot in the front row, clutching a clipboard piled with papers. His face looked taut and, Ava suddenly realized, tired. She watched him for a few moments as he parried the continual onslaught of requests and problems that everyone brought to him. Ava felt an unexpected surge of sympathy. He was trying very hard. She took a big gulp from her cup.

Okay, she thought. *I suppose I can dance around the stage if that's what he wants. If it will make him happy.* She smiled to herself and looked up on the stage. Brad, Jason, and Heather were up there. Ava frowned. *Am I supposed to be up there*, she wondered. She hadn't heard Troy call her name. But when she turned in his direction again she saw he was looking at her expectantly.

"Oh," she said. "Sorry. Here I go." She rose and hurried up the stage steps, noticing when she got there that she was still holding her coffee cup. She looked around for a place to put it down, then, finding none, chugged the rest before putting the empty cup on the floor by the footlights. When she stood she saw Troy watching her. She gave him a little smile. "Sorry," she said.

"That's okay. Everybody ready now?"

Ava nodded enthusiastically. She saw Nigel sitting next to Troy and he gave her a thumbs up sign. Ava smiled broadly, filled with goodwill and hot coffee, ready to rock.

"All right, let's work on Act Three, Scene Two, the fight scene. Take it from Lysander and Helena's entrance," said Troy.

Jason walked to the wing and Ava followed him. Then he looked at her, waiting. "You should go first, don't you think? Since I'm supposed to be chasing you?"

"Oh right!" Ava smacked her forehead. "Duh," she said, and shook her head. "Okay. Here I go."

She strode out onto the stage swinging her arms and wiggling her hips like a speed walker. Jason hastened to catch up. " 'Why should you think that I should woo in scorn,' " he began.

Ava glared at him, tapping her foot. While he continued speaking she turned and faced the audience, rolling her eyes and throwing her hands up in disbelief. Then, fidgeting like a wind-up doll whose spring is near the limit, she turned toward Jason. As soon as he finished his last line Ava's eyes blazed and she seemed to inflate like a bird of prey as she snarled, " 'You do advance your cunning more and more, When truth kills truth, O devilish-holy fray!' "

As she spoke she advanced on Jason, poking him in the chest with her finger with each accusation, her voice swelling with rage. She began circling Jason, who pivoted on the spot trying to keep his eyes on her as she orbited him faster and faster until with her last line she pushed him harder and he lost his balance and fell to the floor.

"Wow!" whispered Troy to Nigel. "What did you say to her?"

"I just gave her a cup of Plan B," whispered Nigel smugly.

"What do you mean?" hissed Troy, not taking his eyes off the stage where Jason was on his knees beseeching Helena to believe him.

"You know, a little liquid courage, as we call it," whispered Nigel.

"You spiked her coffee?"

"Yeah. A cup of rum works wonders, no? Look at her go!" said Nigel.

On stage Ava had just dismissed Lysander's plea with a broad sweep of her arm which caught Jason on the side of his head and knocked him flat. Rubbing his head Jason righted himself and scowled at Ava as he said, " 'Demetrius loves not her, he loves you.' "

This being Brad's cue, he sat up from the sleeping position he had held and began, " 'O Helena, goddess, nymph, perfect divine.' "

As he went on singing her praises Ava spun, crouched, swirled, and feigned choking. Out in the seats Nigel snickered and Troy looked stunned.

Seeing Ava transformed into a whirling Ninja, Troy felt his heart beating faster. There was something unsettling and sexy about the way she moved.

Ava was on fire. " 'O spite! O hell! I see all are bent to set against me for your merriment.' " She continued her outraged lament, charging back and forth across the stage like a missile in search of a target. She was incandescent. She felt great. She looked out and saw Troy staring at her wide-eyed and her pulse raced and she thought, *You want action Boy-Troy? You got it!* And swinging freely she felled Heather with a single wild backhand.

Drawn by the thumping sound of bodies falling, the fairies and mechanicals clustered in the wings and watched Ava. When she tripped Demetrius and he sailed a few feet in the air before thudding to the floor a couple of the fairies applauded. By the time the scene finished Heather and Jason and Brad were eyeing Ava cautiously, edging around at a safe distance while she happily finished her lines.

Troy stood up and applauded when she finished. "That was great Ava. That's what I want to see. You could actually bring it down just a notch. Are you okay, Hermia?" Heather nodded moodily.

"Let's see if we can keep that level of energy in this scene. That's what it needs," said Troy.

"No problem," said Ava, saluting somewhat goofily.

Troy sat down and spoke to Nigel quietly. "I appreciate that you were trying to help. And obviously it worked. But don't ever do it again, understand?"

Nigel smirked. "You think she can flame like that without fuel? I don't."

Troy looked at Ava, her black hair glossy in the stage light, her face flushed and shining and he felt undeniably aroused. He didn't want to admit that he had his doubts too.

* * *

The next day Ava woke up with a headache. A shrieking wind rattled the screens on her windows and assaulted her as soon as she stepped outside. *Shoot. I have got to find those car keys*, she thought, wrapping her windbreaker closer. She set off into the gale, heading toward Starbucks. As she walked she thought about the wonderful coffee Nigel had given her the night before. *I've got to ask him where his café is*, she thought, remembering the pretty moon and stars cup.

By the time she reached the coffee shop the wind had whipped Ava's normally sleek hair into a punk rock statement fit for The Cure. She shivered with relief as she stepped up to place her order. As she turned around to wait she saw Troy reading a newspaper in one of the chairs by the window. He hadn't noticed her, and Ava felt an impulse to slip away before he did. But she couldn't leave without her coffee.

Come on, Ave, she thought. *Just say hello. Be nice.*

Before she could make up her mind Troy looked up from his paper and right into her eyes. Ava attempted a smile, but the odd expression on Troy's face puzzled her. She ran a hand up to her hair and suddenly felt self-conscious. Then he smiled, and she felt strangely shy. She grabbed her coffee as it was placed on the counter and Troy stood up and said, "Hi. Won't you sit with me for a minute?"

"I . . ." Ava began to beg off, but seeing the warmth in Troy's eyes she softened and said, "Okay. I've only got a few minutes."

He looked at her with that funny expression again and Ava said, "What? Is it my hair? It's a mess, I know. The wind . . ."

"No. I mean, the wind is incredible, but your hair looks fine. I mean. I like it that way. You look like one of those Japanese anime cartoons."

"The kids with the big eyes?"

"Yeah. And the spiky hair."

Ava smiled. She'd never thought of herself that way.

"Well, thanks. I guess. I think I'm a little taller than most of them though."

Troy smiled at her. "I wanted to tell you how great you were last night."

"You think so?"

"Definitely. I really liked the way you took charge of the scene. It's much stronger that way than having Helena be some kind of victim."

Ava nodded. "I'm glad. I don't know what came over me. It just felt right to be angry, for her to be angry I mean."

Troy's expression clouded. He took a breath and then spoke rapidly.

"Um. Listen Ava, I hope you won't get upset but there's something you should know about last night."

Ava tilted her head to one side, watching Troy. "What?" she said.

Troy frowned slightly. "I feel kind of responsible since I had asked Nigel to help you get the right feel for Helena."

"You told Nigel to talk to me?" Ava interrupted, unable to keep the irritation out of her voice.

Troy nodded. "I just asked him if he could help you work on bringing out Helena's character."

Ava pursed her lips. "Let me guess. Because he's British, right? So naturally that makes him an expert on Shakespeare. Silly me. Why didn't I think of that?"

Troy grew serious. "Listen Ava. I know you want to do well in this play, and, well, it just seemed to me that you didn't want to take any direction from me, so I thought maybe you would listen if it came from someone else."

Ava's breaths began coming more rapidly. Her head was splitting and now this patronizing twerp was telling her she couldn't take direction.

"I think it's pretty clear that I can take direction, considering last night," she said icily.

Troy grimaced slightly and said, "Well, about last night . . ."

Ava's eyes widened, watching Troy stroke his chin as if

searching for the right phrase. "What? What about last night? I was good. You said so yourself."

"Yes, well. I think the reason you may have been so good had something to do with the coffee Nigel gave you."

Ava stared at him blankly.

"It had a cup of rum in it."

"What! It was really sweet, but I would have noticed that much alcohol."

"Well, maybe the coffee was really strong. Listen, I want you to know I had no idea Nigel was going to pull something like that and as soon as he told me I warned him never to do anything like that again, but I felt you should know."

Ava sat stunned. Her head throbbed. *No wonder*, she thought darkly.

"That little creep," she muttered. "I'm going to kill him."

"Now Ava, I know you're mad, and you have every right to be. But just remember how great you were last night. Remember? I'll never forget how shocked Brad was when you tripped him and sent him flying. That was great stuff."

Ava frowned and stared out the window at the sunlight glaring off the Kinko's sign. After a moment of charged silence she said, "So, I'm only good when I'm loaded. Is that what you're saying?"

"No. Not at all. I think maybe the alcohol helped you to tap into the power you keep inside. I think now that you've felt it, and used it, you'll be able to find it again. Without any 'coffee.'"

Ava glared sullenly at the newspaper lying between them. Above them Frank Sinatra's voice crooned on the sound system, "It was just one of those things." *Right*, thought Ava. *I see how it is.*

Her jaw set and her eyes hard, she gathered up her things and said, "Fine. I'll see you tonight I guess. And you can tell Nigel how much I appreciate his help. But if he tries anything like that again I'll crush him like a bug."

Ava swept out and Troy watched her go, feeling incredibly turned on. *God, she's hot when she's angry*, he thought.

Chapter Six

In the weeks which followed Ava's flaming scene, re-hearsals continued with the stop and start rhythm of an office elevator. Different sets of people kept getting up on the stage and getting off, fitting their lines and movements together slowly, and in some cases painfully.

Ava began having elevator dreams, going up and down all night, and each time the door opened there would be another long hallway with no exit. Just another elevator to get into. She woke each morning exhausted.

Jason, Brad, and Heather had lodged a formal complaint with Troy about Ava's over-the-top slapstick and Troy had asked her to hold back, at least until Hell Week, the last week of rehearsals.

Since learning of Nigel's deception, Ava had pointedly ignored him, and the Brit's attempts at creating an alliance against her with some of the other players had backfired. The fairies, in particular, had adopted Ava as their champion after seeing how she handled Brad, Jason, and Heather, whose self-centered whining and lack of professionalism had earned them the disdain of most of the cast.

Adding to the growing friction on the set was the open hostility between Marion and Howard, whose lovers' tiff as

Titania and Oberon was nothing compared to the contempt they seemed to feel for one another offstage.

Ava was puzzled by the animosity until Aram Feingold, who played Peter Quince, told her how Howard had been insulted by Marion's critique of his performance and had retaliated by suggesting she was too old for the part of Queen of the Fairies.

For her part, Ava was surprised to discover that she was beginning to look forward to the ripple of laughter that rewarded her when she delivered a line well, or when she executed a bit of slapstick burlesque. She had never realized how much fun it could be to make people laugh. It was a different kind of power, and she was energized by it. She found herself looking forward to the scenes where she knew she could make things happen.

By mid-April when the rains began, tension was palpable in the theatre, and it only got worse when the smokers in the cast were driven in by the rains and began lighting up backstage whenever they thought they could get away with it. The non-smokers, worried about their stage voices, complained to Troy.

Beset by worries about cost overruns on the costumes and sets, and concerns about the leaks in the theatre's aged roof, Troy tried to mute the discord. He had more immediate concerns.

Midway through April, only two weeks before opening night, one of the fairies quit abruptly, claiming he couldn't waste his time on rehearsals anymore with final exams nearing. Troy was considering doing without the extra fairy as he watched his son play in a soccer game Saturday morning when a brilliant solution occurred to him.

In the truck on the way to lunch after the game Troy waited until Josh had finished his usual bubbling post-game wrap. Then he said, "Hey Josh, I have a favor to ask, buddy."

Josh looked at him, mildly curious.

Troy cleared his throat. "It's like this. You know my play? Remember how there are some fairies in my play?"

"Yeah," said Josh flatly, looking out the window.

"Well, one of my fairies had to quit. Because he's a student and he has exams coming up, and anyway, I need to find someone who can take his place."

"Yeah?" Josh glanced briefly at his father, barely paying attention.

"Well, the thing is, I was wondering if you could help me out."

Josh's small brow furrowed.

Troy hurried on, "You could play the part Josh. You wouldn't have to say any lines. You'd just be running around on the stage when the rest of the fairies do their thing. It would be fun. And then you could be with me on Friday and Saturday nights when I have to be at the theatre."

Since weekend rehearsals had intensified, Troy had struggled to find places for Josh to be each weekend, but he wasn't about to ask his former wife for help.

Josh frowned and said, "Would I have to wear something stupid? I thought only girls are fairies."

Troy inhaled carefully, "Well, no. Actually, men and boys can be fairies too. There's even a king of the fairies in the play."

Josh looked doubtful.

Troy turned into the parking space by his apartment building and stopped the engine. "Listen Josh, I know you're not a theatre guy. But it would really help me out if you could do this. And we could be together."

"Couldn't I just stay with Carlos? Or Aunt Jenny?"

"Aunt Jenny has been taking care of you for weeks now Josh. I can't keep asking her. Or Carlos either."

Josh sighed and kicked his foot against the soccer ball at his feet. Then, he said, "Okay. I guess."

Troy sighed with relief. "Great. That's great. It'll be fun. You can start tonight."

Josh opened the truck door and hopped down. He kicked the soccer ball ahead of him and followed it looking pensive.

Troy watched him with a sinking feeling. And, it had just

occurred to him, his ex-wife probably wasn't going to think much of the idea of her son being a fairy. *Hah. Deal with it*, thought Troy.

A few hours later, carrying a fragrant hot pizza box, Troy and Josh entered the theatre. With set construction underway, Troy spent every free moment at the theatre to make sure the volunteer crew followed his instructions.

He parked Josh at a card table backstage and went off to consult with the carpenters.

"Hey, that smells great. Can I have some?"

Josh looked up, his mouth smeared with orange grease, and saw an older boy smiling at him. He was wearing a black PlayStation t-shirt.

"I've got that game," said Josh.

The boy looked down at his shirt. "Oh, this. Yeah. I like the new game better though. Better sound board."

Josh nodded thoughtfully. "Yeah."

The boy sat down in the chair next to Josh and said, "So, about this pizza?"

"Sure. 'Cept save some for my dad. It's his dinner too."

"Your dad? Oh, you're Troy's kid? Cool. Your dad's a good guy."

Josh nodded, his mouth full.

"You come to watch, eh?"

"Nah. My dad asked me to be a fairy 'cause some guy quit."

"Really! You're gonna take Jeremy's place? That's great! We'll have fun. Being a fairy's the best. I'm a fairy. You get to goof off all the time and play cards and stuff."

"Yeah?"

"Oh yeah. Plus, you get to hang out with all the pretty girls."

Josh shrugged. "I guess."

The boy smiled and said, "My name's Alex."

"I'm Josh."

"Tell me Josh, do you know how to play seven card stud?"

Josh looked curious. "No. What is it?"

Alex grinned and pulled a deck of cards from his pocket. "It's the best card game there is. I'll show you."

An hour later the grease on the top of the pizza had soaked through the box and four more players had found spots at the table.

"Prithee, I call thy bluff and raise thee a dime."

"Ha, ha, read them and weep Mustardseed."

The sound of the fairies at play drew Ava to the game and she looked at Josh studying his cards and said, "Hi guys. Who's your friend?"

"Fair Helena, give glad greetings to our newest fairy, Moth by name, though some mortals do call him Josh," said Alex.

Josh met Ava's eyes gravely and nodded.

"Hello Moth," said Ava, looking slightly confused. "Are you, is he, someone's brother?"

"He's Troy's kid," said Iris, grinning like a cat wearing black-lined purple lipstick. "Jeremy quit. So Josh's gonna help us out, aren't you Josh?"

Josh nodded again.

Ava looked at his blonde tousled hair and ocean gray eyes and she thought, *I'll bet Troy looked just like that when he was little.*

"Hey, any of that pizza left?"

Troy came up behind Josh and Ava saw how the boy's face lit up at the sound of his voice.

"We saved you two pieces, Dad. But they're cold," he said.

"Two cold pieces, eh? Well, I guess that'll have to do," said Troy, smiling at Ava.

Although Ava had not forgiven Troy for his role in the Nigel/coffee incident, she had been finding it harder to maintain her chilly distance as the weeks went by. Troy worked harder than anyone else. He was there before everyone and stayed long after they left and she knew he was working long hours at his real job now that spring was in high gear. The working man's tan on his face and forearms looked good on him and more and more Ava found herself staring in his direction when she needed a lift. She really didn't know why.

So, when he lifted one of the limp slices from the box and said to her, "Have you eaten, Ava?" she laughed and said, "Yes, thanks. I think you need it more than I do."

Troy looked at her. Ava met his eyes and felt a shudder of energy that had nothing to do with the play. He carried his cold pizza over to where she stood and said in a low voice, "Won't you at least keep me company while I enjoy this?"

She laughed and followed him to an empty row of theater seats away from the crowd. He ate quickly and quietly, as if trying to get it out of the way.

"Hey, didn't your mother ever tell you not to gobble your food?" said Ava.

Troy smiled as he wiped the grease off his chin. "My mother wasn't exactly a great cook."

"Neither is mine, but she always said that the most important thing about a meal is the time you take to eat it. It's the time that is important. That slowing down, sharing a few moments with whoever."

Troy studied Ava's face. "Maybe I just haven't been with the right person to make me want to slow down before."

Ava felt a warmth spreading in her chest. She looked down and said quickly, "You know, I know I haven't been all that easy to work with during these past few months, but, it's really meant a lot to me, doing this play. And I think you're doing a wonderful job."

She looked up and Troy's eyes were staring at her intently, as if trying to see inside her. "I'm glad you feel that way. I know you were . . . not happy at the start."

Ava shook her head. "I didn't know . . . I've never actually been in a play before. I didn't realize how time consuming it is. How much . . ."

"How much work it takes?"

"Yeah, that's part of it." She lifted her hands in a gesture of wordless gratitude. "But it's also . . . I've learned so much. You were so right about the part. I never knew how much fun it could be to make people laugh."

"Wait till you hear them applaud," said Troy, his eyes shining darkly at her. "The first play I was in, I was just a guy in the chorus of *The Music Man*. I didn't have a single line of my own, but I had to be there for every rehearsal, and before opening night I knew every line in the whole play. And it was the most fun I'd ever had. It didn't matter that I didn't have a big part. It was just great to be a part of the show. That's when I learned that theatre is kind of like life— it's not about what part you play, it's about how you play your part. No matter how small it is. And that's when I first learned how in every show the cast and crew get to be like this strange family. You get to know people you'd never meet in your regular life, and you get to share this amazing thing with them."

Ava smiled. "Yes. I'm beginning to see that. I feel like Tim Murphy is the big brother I never had."

"You never had a big brother?"

"I'm an only child."

"Aah. So this theatre family is really new for you, then."

"Yes. And I'm loving it."

"I'm glad." Troy paused and a shade of concern came into his expression. "Just don't forget that it's make-believe."

"What do you mean?"

"I mean, when the play's over, all these people will go their separate ways. Maybe you'll see some of them again. Maybe you'll even be in another play with some of them. But the special family that we are now will vanish." Troy hesitated. "Sometimes it's hard to say goodbye to people you've become so close to."

Ava felt him looking at her intently and she felt a strange urge to reach out and touch him, but she restrained herself. What would he think?

The screech of the auditorium door ruptured the mood, especially as it was immediately echoed by the even more resonant shriek of Marion bearing down the aisle in full sail. Behind her Nina tacked like a tugboat trying for purchase.

"Please Marion," she kept saying. "I'm sure he didn't mean it. If you'll just calm down Marion . . ."

"Calm down? I am calmed down," shouted Marion. "If I weren't able to control my anger Howard would be dead by now."

"Please Marion. Let's sit down with Troy and we'll figure out a way to make Howard stop being such an idiot."

"Hah! The only way to make that man stop being such an idiot would be to murder him. I refuse to lower myself to his level. If he thinks he can go around calling me a washed-out hag in the newspapers then he had better get himself a good lawyer is all I have to say."

Troy stood at the edge of the stage and Nina looked up at him and rolled her eyes while Marion flounced into a seat. Troy came down off the stage and sat next to Marion and said quietly, "Can you tell me what's going on Marion?"

"What's going on is I am going to have to quit if someone doesn't make it clear to Howard that he owes me a public apology. A public apology! I will not accept some mumbled lie from that ape. He has to go find that reporter and get her to print a retraction or that's it. I'm finished with this two-bit production. I'm sorry, Troy. I don't hold you entirely responsible. You couldn't have known the man would turn out to be such a fool." Marion hugged her bag of knitting to her chest and glared out at the stage heaving slightly like a ruffled hen after a narrow escape from the local fox.

"Uh, Nina, can you explain?" Troy said quietly.

Nina leaned her head close to Troy and said in an undertone, "It's in today's *Dispatch*. Apparently Howard had a drink with some reporter last night and got a little above himself and now we're left holding the bag."

"Have you seen the article?"

"No. But judging by Marion's reaction, it can't be good."

Troy shook his head and closed his eyes. Nina looked at him sympathetically. She put a hand on his shoulder and said, "I know, I know. It's just one thing after another. That's show biz. Don't worry. Marion's a trouper. She'll calm down. We just have to make Howard toe the line."

Troy looked up on the stage where all the fairies and Ava and his son were standing, watching. "Okay, everyone, let's get to work. We have a show to do."

"Hmmph," said Marion.

Troy crouched next to her and said softly, "Marion, I will make this right. I promise."

Marion breathed deeply and didn't say anything for a moment. Then she lifted her chin and said, "I will not let you down, Troy. You know that. But I wouldn't rely on that beast if I were you."

"Thank you Marion." Troy stood up. He turned and looked at the stage, where the crew were assembling a forest of gauzy trees and ferns against a shimmering backdrop Troy had spent two days painting to look like a misty moonlit sky. Despite his worries Troy had to smile. It was starting to look magical. And there was Ava laughing with Alex and Iris and Josh. Troy was startled as he felt the clutch of desire in his gut. She towered over the other three. But he didn't care. She looked like a supermodel in her silken jade top and skinny black jeans. Ava was radiant.

"You all right?" Troy looked down. Nina was looking up at him anxiously. "You look like you're kind of spacing out there," she said.

Troy shook himself slightly. "No. No, I'm fine. Just thinking." He paused. "The set's coming along."

"Yeah. It's looking great," agreed Nina. Without thinking she glanced up at the ceiling and noticed a spreading dark patch that looked suspiciously wet above the stage. *Oh hell*, she thought, *one darn thing after another*.

Chapter Seven

A ray of dancing sunlight flickered across Ava's desk late the next afternoon and her heart lifted with hope that she might get a chance to go for a run after work. Troy had given the cast a rare night off to allow the tech crew to finish setting up the lights and sound equipment.

Chenille's head poked in the door.

"Pick you up at six forty-five?"

Ava frowned. "Oh? Oh! Oh right. I'm sorry Nille. I had totally forgotten. I've been so busy."

Chenille looked concerned. "If you don't want to go . . ."

"No. No, I want to go. It will be fun, I'm sure," said Ava, sure only that it couldn't be any worse than it usually was. The annual EM (English Major) dinner held each year at the home of one of the deans, offered a chance for the wits and bores to gather like members of some dying tribe participating in blood sacrifices to gods everyone knew were dead but everyone still worshipped out of habit or envy.

Chenille always enjoyed the events for the chance to dress up and flirt with the relatively exotic visiting professors. Ava went along to provide cover for Chenille, and to humor her friend's eternally romantic delusion that The Right Man would inevitably be on the guest list some day.

"Wow! You look great," said Chenille when Ava opened her apartment door. Ava had decided to go with her old faithful, the little black dress, a slender spill of chiffon with feather straps, silver coils in her hair, and two-inch black heels. The heels, in complete disregard of her mother's constant advice, Ava wore because she loved the way they looked, they made her feel sexy, and she figured if any guy was put off by her height, another two inches wasn't going to matter.

Chenille was swathed in cobalt blue crepe, plunging low to reveal her creamy cleavage, and a string of blue glass beads sparkled at her neck. Even though the guest list at these dinners never wavered—always the same dull married professors, the same self-absorbed singles, and the small group of patronizing visiting scholars, Chenille approached each dinner as if it might be the one where eyes would meet across a crowded room and her life would be transported to some higher, sweeter plane. It was one of the things Ava loved about her.

Ava herself had fewer illusions about the romantic potential of the evening. Her goals were more modest. Eat, drink, and get the hell out of there without being trapped into some stupefyingly tedious discussion of some arcane literary debate.

When they arrived, Ava accepted a glass of white wine and walked over to the edge of a cluster of professors who seemed to be arguing over the legitimacy of film adaptations of Shakespeare, in particular, Baz Luhrmann's rock and roll version of *Romeo and Juliet*.

Ava was listening quietly without feeling engaged at all when she was startled out of her passive stance by the sound of someone speaking her name.

"Ava, what do you think?" asked Gerald Hopkins, Dean of the English department. Gerald turned to the group and said, "Ava's taking part in a local production of *Midsummer Night's Dream*."

"Oh really? What fun Ava!" said Maude Renk, a squat loud-voiced woman who was also a Milton scholar with a famously bawdy outlook. "We'll all have to come see you."

"What part are you playing Ava?" asked Wilson Spiggot, chair of classical studies.

"I'm Helena."

"Oh," said Maude, with a perplexed look. "Isn't she one of the young ones? The lovers?"

Ava smiled thinly and opened her mouth but before she could speak a clipped baritone announced, "Helena's a rotten part."

This pronouncement fell like a rock in the conversational pool, a ring of silence widening around it till Wilson graciously jumped in with, "Oh I'm sure nothing Ava does could be rotten."

Ava smiled at him gratefully, at the same time searching out the source of the nasty comment. Her gaze fell on a pair of dark blue eyes smoldering from under heavy brows. His hair was black, slicked back like some silent film star, and to top it off, he had a small black mustache in the center of his chiseled features. Ava was utterly repelled, even though a part of her mind registered that, to his credit, he seemed to be at least two or three inches taller than she was.

She fixed him with a look and said, "What makes you say that?"

Maude stepped forward rather officiously between them and said, "Ava, I don't think you've met our visiting Cambridge scholar, Ainsley Wolfe? He's published two books on Bacon."

"Really?" said Ava. "And of course, being British, I guess you can tell us all about what Shakespeare really meant?"

Ainsley's lips curved slightly upward. "Of course, it's wonderful that you Americans take such pleasure in performing Shakespeare's works. It's just a pity that you don't have the resources or the training to enable you to do it properly."

He paused to share a smile with the group. "As for Helena, well, I think it's obvious isn't it? She falls into that useful but somehow regrettable category of Shakespeare's clowns, like the nurse in *Romeo and Juliet*. The ungainly female who furthers the plot through her misguided efforts. A necessary role, perhaps, but not a particularly poetic one. A woman as lovely as you, Ava, should be cast in a role with more dignity."

Ava clenched her fists and gritted her teeth, determined not to show this snob how furious she was. Plus, he had the gall to flatter her at the same time that he insulted all Americans! Gaaa. She screamed at him inside, but on the surface, she maintained a diplomatic calm. "Well. Thank you, I guess. If that was a compliment. Personally, I'm glad to be playing Helena. She's a fighter and she's not afraid to go after what she wants. And she certainly isn't about to let any man tell her how to do it."

Ava stared coolly at Ainsley, daring him to disagree. In the back of her mind she suddenly remembered how Troy had described the role of Helena to her as the best one in the play and she felt an unfamiliar glow of pride that was somehow connected to him.

At that moment Chenille tugged at Ava's elbow and steered her away.

"Hey, are you okay? You look like you swallowed something the wrong way."

Ava snorted. "I'm all right. What a creep!"

A scent of lime cologne drifted near and a low voice with a clipped accent said, "We're not all that obnoxious."

Ava turned and found herself looking into a pair of gray eyes alight with amusement. His shoulder length blonde hair framed a lean face, and he was looking down on her from an advantage of several inches. Ava felt her anger softening.

"Oh David, I didn't know you'd be here." Chenille beamed at Ava. "This is David Taylor, our classics scholar. He's on loan from Cambridge for this year. We're all so excited to have him here."

"You're too kind," said David, smiling at Ava.

"Ava teaches art history," Chenille added, in her best matchmaker tone.

"Hello," said Ava, shaking David's hand, which was cool and strong, she noticed.

"I must apologize for Ainsley. He can be a bit of a twit," said David.

Ava smiled. "Well, I'm sure he means well."

"Oh, I wouldn't be so sure," said David.

Ava laughed.

They went in to dinner, and although Ava still had an urge to throw her drink at Ainsley, she realized, seeing him at the far end of the table, he was probably out of range. Also, with David at her side providing sly sarcastic commentary all through dinner, Ava found it easier to forget the other Brit.

In the pause between the main course and dessert, however, as Ava listened to the various threads of discussion, with learned scholars defending or dissecting small points of literary interest on all sides of her, she felt a curious wave of detachment from the entire crowd. They were all so full of themselves. She had a sudden vision of Troy, so self-effacing, yet so quietly energetic and creative. Ava couldn't imagine him fitting in with this crowd of self-satisfied wits, yet she could think of no one whom she respected more.

She came out of her reverie at the sound of Chenille's laughter. Ava smiled. At least Chenille was enjoying herself.

As the coffee was being poured Ava looked across the table and noticed a bearded man with twinkling copper eyes looking at her sympathetically. Meeting her glance, he leaned across and said in an undertone flavored with a thick Scottish accent, "Ainsley's an expert at being an expert. Don't let him bother you. I'm sure you're going to be grand as Helena."

Ava smiled and felt her shoulders relaxing. "Thank you," she said quietly, noticing that the bearded man seemed to be including Chenille in his extended goodwill. But when Ava glanced at Chenille she seemed stiff and uncomfortable. Ava looked back at the bearded man, who shrugged slightly and grinned, leaving Ava more puzzled than before.

On the way home Ava confronted Chenille. "So what's with the bearded guy and you?"

"Nothing! There is and there will be nothing between me and the bearded guy," said Chenille, gripping the steering wheel a little tighter.

"Really? He seemed nice to me."

"Yeah, well. You're such a big connoisseur of nice guys."

"Who is he?"

"His name is Fergus McMillan. He teaches comp lit."

"And?"

"And nothing."

"Nille. This isn't like you. That's how I know it's not nothing. Did you go out with him?"

"I did not. He asked me. But it just isn't going to work."

"Why not? He's got that cool Scottish accent thing, like Sean Connery."

Chenille frowned and turned to Ava briefly. "Yes. But he's got a beard."

Ava stared at her. "Are you saying, that's a deal breaker?"

Chenille took a deep breath. "Okay. I'm not proud of it, but yes, since you ask, that's a deal breaker."

"You're a beardist?"

Chenille tried not to smile. "Yes. It's true. I am a beardist."

Ava laughed. "But Nille. That's ridiculous. You could ask him to shave it off."

"Oh right. I'll just say, sure I'll go out with you as long as you shave off that bush on your chin? I don't think so. What if a man said, I'll go out with you if you dye your hair blonde? Or I'll go out with you if you lose weight? It can't be done."

Ava shook her head. "Man. And I thought I had problems."

"Like what?"

Ava stopped smiling and looked out the window thoughtfully for a minute. "Well, I can't exactly ask Troy to grow a foot can I?"

Chenille stopped at Ava's apartment building. "No. No, I guess you can't."

Ava hugged Chenille and got out. The rain was starting again and the sidewalks shone in the streetlights. In some parallel universe she could be looking forward to a night of hot passion with her director. But not tonight, she sighed.

The steady drumming of rain on the roof of his truck forced Troy to turn up his radio. He wanted to catch the forecast, though he had a gloomy feeling that he already knew what it would be. It hadn't rained *every* minute of the last two weeks. There had been a few periods where it was only gray and drizzly, and a couple of teasing breaks in the cloud cover, but these slight respites had done little to diminish the feeling of being on the losing end of a Super Soaker battle.

And as quickly as that memory hit Troy, of laughing and rolling in the wet grass with Josh, he had an inspiration for a way to reduce the steadily increasing tension among the cast members. He would schedule a team-building picnic and casual soccer game for the entire cast and crew this Sunday, the last free day before Hell Week. Troy smiled at the thought. If nothing else, it would give him a chance to kick some soccer balls with Josh, and it would be good for everyone to take a day off before the last hard push. He just had to pray the rains would let up for the weekend.

When he got to the theatre Troy announced his idea. It met with mixed emotions. The fairies were totally down with it, as were Jason, Brad, and Heather, who as a matter of collegial pride welcomed any excuse to avoid rehearsal. The mechanicals scoffed at the concept of team-building as new age corporate baloney, but they liked the picnic component. Howard and Nigel claimed indifference, though Nigel took the opportunity to mention that he had grown up playing football, as all the rest of the world calls soccer.

"I hardly think it's a good use of our precious time to go outside and play in the mud when we should be working," said Marion. Her knitting needles never paused while she delivered this opinion, but when a vote was taken and the majority favored a day in the park, Marion just sighed and set her lips in a thin line, going on record as the one dissenting vote.

Ava raised her hand. After years in the classroom she did it without even thinking. Troy smiled when he noticed and said, "Yes, Ava?"

"Do you want us all to bring food for the picnic? I mean, should we all bring something to share, or just do our own thing?"

"Share!" "Share!" "Share!" The fairies and the mechanicals lobbied loudly and the plan was set.

Nigel raised his hand. Troy's smile vanished. "Yes, Nigel?"

"What if it rains?"

Troy hesitated. "Well. If it rains, I guess we come here and work as usual. But we could still bring our picnic food and have a picnic indoors."

In the silence that followed Marion's knitting needles clicked a Morse code message of disapproval.

"All right, then. It's settled. Let's get to work."

The next day when they met for lunch, Ava told Chenille about the picnic and asked her advice.

"You're a much better cook than I am Nille. What should I bring?"

"That depends. Who are you trying to impress? The studly fairy king? The sensitive director? Or you could just pick up something at the Q-Mart."

"No. I want to bring something nice."

Chenille studied Ava's face for a minute. "So how are things between you and Troy?"

"What's that got to do with the food at the picnic?"

"Well, you know, the way to a man's heart and all that. Food, I mean," Chenille said before taking a big bite out of her vegan sub.

"I'm not trying to impress anybody. It's just a picnic, okay? But I don't want to just bring a bag of chips."

"Hmm." Chenille thought for minute while she chewed.

Ava pushed her pasta salad around on her plate and said, "I was thinking about maybe a fruit salad. Except there's not much fresh fruit right now."

Chenille nodded. "But you know, that might be a good idea. Isn't there a place in the play where Titania recites a grocery list for the fairies to gather for Bottom? I seem to recall 'apricocks' figured into it."

Ava stabbed a black olive with her fork. "Yeah. That's right. She mentions apricocks and green figs, purple grapes and dewberries, whatever they are."

"See. I knew it. You can put together a Fairy Fruit Salad. It would be yummy and also clever. I'm sure Troy would be impressed."

"I doubt it," said Ava, but she thought it would be fun to do anyway.

At least it had seemed like a good idea until Saturday morning when she finally got a chance to go shopping for the fruits. *Honestly,* she thought. *Doesn't anyone sell fresh fruit in this town?* After an hour of fruitless searching at her usual markets she tracked down some outrageously expensive fresh apricots, some hard green figs, some reddish grapes, and some canned gooseberries, which she planned to palm off as dewberries. She also bought a few California strawberries just because she couldn't resist and when she had finished assembling the salad it looked pretty and appealing and she began to look forward to the picnic.

It would be the first time she would be socializing with the cast outside the theatre, and Ava worried a little that it would be like an office party, where everyone stands around awkwardly out of context. In fact, when she woke up Sunday morning and heard the thunder rumbling like a trash truck in the distance she almost felt relieved, thinking the picnic would be moved into the theatre. But by the time she took a shower and balanced her checkbook the sun was glinting on puddles outside.

At the park a dozen or so of the tech crew and a few of the fairies were kicking around a soccer ball when Ava got there.

Troy waved from a table set up under a tree where people were putting the food.

"Oh this looks so nice. This was a really good idea," she said to Troy as she placed her bowl on the table.

"Wow, that looks good. I love fruit salad," he said.

Ava smiled. "I made it with all the fruits Titania mentions when she tells the fairies to feed Bottom."

"Really? So, then you must know what dewberries are huh?"

"Well sure. Doesn't everybody?"

Troy looked at her for a second, then smiled. "Everybody but me, I guess."

Ava smiled. "Just between you and me, I haven't a clue. But I decided that gooseberries were weird enough to qualify. Although, Nigel will probably quibble."

"Just so he doesn't eat it all."

Josh ran up wearing his cleats and a DC United shirt that hung almost to his knees. "Hey Dad, come on. We've almost got two teams now. You have to be on my team."

Troy caught Ava's eye over Josh's head and said, "Okay. Be right there."

Josh darted off and Troy said in a different tone, "Are you going to play?"

Ava pulled back slightly. She had worn her running shoes, but had no intention of getting involved in any soccer playing.

"Um, no. I think I'll just watch. I'll cheer for you."

At this Troy smiled softly and said, "I'll try to win for you."

And he ran off leaving Ava feeling oddly giddy. She watched Troy gather with his teammates and her heart hummed steadily. Ava recognized the tune, but she pretended not to hear it. *He's still too short,* she told her heart. But it went on humming just the same.

Sizing up the other players, Ava noticed that nearly half of them were women, including, to her surprise, Heather, looking very athletic in her soccer shorts and close-fitting lycra top. The women on the field seemed to Ava's inexperienced eyes to be equally skilled as the men and boys.

A brighter shade of green arrested Ava's glance and she saw Marion moving slowly toward the picnic area. She was shading herself with a white umbrella and wearing lime green Capri pants and white Keds. She reminded Ava of Ginger on Gilligan's Island, although, perhaps an older, wiser Ginger as a result of being washed up in the backwaters of Richmond rather than the alternate universe of endless television reruns.

"Well, isn't this just lovely," said Marion, setting a plate of asparagus spears on the table.

"Yes. We're so lucky the rain stopped," said Ava.

They watched the game for a few minutes without speaking. Ava couldn't help noticing how gracefully Troy ran, and how deftly he manipulated the ball ricocheting around on the wet grass.

"I've never understood this game," said Marion, after another minute. "It just looks to me like they're running up and down kicking the ball. Are there rules? How does someone win?"

Ava turned a bemused look on Marion, whose dramatic pale face was half covered by her enormous sunglasses. "I don't know much about the game either, really. I tried to play it when I was a teenager but it's kind of fast moving and I never got the hang of it. I always felt like I was in the middle of a pinball machine."

Marion nodded. "I don't understand. Why doesn't someone just pick up the ball and run with it for a touchdown?"

Ava smiled. "That's football."

"Isn't that what this is? I thought football and soccer were the same game." Marion frowned slightly and stepped back as a couple of players went sprinting past, their sneakers squishing loudly in the soggy grass.

"They are, in Europe. Here soccer is soccer and football is something else."

"I see." Marion watched the game for a few more minutes. "Well, I have to say, it doesn't look all that difficult. The girls seem to manage quite well."

"Yes." Ava put a hand up to shade her eyes, wishing she'd

brought a baseball cap. "That's one of the best things about soccer, I think. That anyone can play. At any age."

Marion headed for the folding chairs and sat down to watch, and after a few more minutes Ava joined her. The spectator section grew slightly as the wives of some of the mechanicals arrived, and Ava began to feel uncomfortable about being lumped with the passive group. The soccer players seemed to be having such fun. She almost wished she were playing, but she didn't want to face Nigel in a contest where he must feel even more superior than usual.

After the game ended the players came over and devoured food with a carefree abandon that made Ava feel even more like the old maid at a party of hyperactive children. She was watching Brad toss grapes into the air and catch most of them in his mouth when she felt a presence behind her.

"Hey, you ought to come play with us in the next game."

Troy was right beside her, kneeling so his eyes were level with hers and she was struck by the quicksilver light in them. His skin was glistening with a light coat of sweat and he smelled like wet grass and sunshine.

"Oh. I'm really a klutz at soccer," she said.

"That's okay. We're just goofing around out there. It's not about the soccer. It's about playing together."

"The team building thing?" said Ava.

"Right. The team building thing."

"But I'm already on the team. I mean. I'm . . ." Ava tried to think of how to say why she didn't want to play, but as she tried to think of an excuse she felt a push of desire to join the players. It did look like fun.

"Well," she hesitated.

"Come on. You can be on my team." Troy touched her arm as he said this and Ava felt a rush of heat go right up to her face. She quickly stood up and said, "Okay. You talked me into it."

Troy smiled and turned to Marion.

"How about you, Marion? You don't have to run if you

don't want to. You can be a defender. Just camp out by the goal and get in the other team's way."

Marion looked puzzled. "You know Troy, I simply don't get this game. I mean it just looks like total chaos to me. Everyone running around every which way. What is the point? How do you know who's winning?"

Troy laughed. "You know what it is, Marion. The thing about soccer is it's not like baseball where everything is scripted and everyone has their parts well defined and their choices are limited. Soccer is like improv. Everyone can make it up as they go along. It's like jazz. So if you get another player who plays in the same rhythm you do, and you can get something going despite the other team trying to mess you up the whole time, then it's beautiful. The Brazilians call it the beautiful game. If you watch it for a while I think you'd get to appreciate it."

Marion looked skeptical, but intrigued.

"Improv, eh?"

"Right. It's just like in improv you try to give the other players something to work with. You do the same thing in soccer. It's give and take, spontaneous. That's what makes it so exciting. It's never the same way twice."

Marion nodded thoughtfully. "Well. Maybe I should try it for a few minutes just to see what all the fuss is about." She stood up slowly and folded up her parasol. "Are we starting now? Who's team am I on? Where do I stand?"

Troy beamed.

When the players finished refueling, which only took a few minutes it seemed to Ava, they regrouped on the field and Ava immediately felt a pang of trepidation seeing both Nigel and Howard on the opposing team. It was probably just her imagination but Nigel did seem to be grinning eagerly, like a cat who has spotted a baby bird fallen on the lawn. Ava set her jaw and determined not to go down without a fight.

Moments later she was racing for the ball, all rational

thought on hold. There was only running, the grass, the clunk of shoes kicking the ball. Ava felt her muscles loosening up and her hair flying as she ran. Then she heard Troy call her name and she looked toward him and saw him kick the ball to her. She focused on the coming ball, running in place to get her feet ready to accept the pass. Suddenly a shoulder slammed into her side and she looked down and saw Heather racing away with the ball. *All right. That's it you little witch*, she thought, and sprinted after Heather with mayhem in her heart.

Ava lost track of the time for the next few minutes until the ball shot behind her and a brace of opponents hurtled past her. Then there was a piercing scream and everyone stopped running and looked to where Marion lay on the grass moaning like a broken cello.

"Ow my leg! My leg! He crushed my leg! You monster! You clumsy jerk!"

Marion's leg was bent at an unnatural angle and a blood red stain was soaking through her capri pants. Howard loomed over her guiltily, looking like the Hulk after a particularly unfortunate episode. "It was an accident," he mumbled. "I was trying to avoid her but she stepped right in front of me."

"He said I was supposed to get in your way," shrieked Marion, pounding the grass with her little fist.

"Someone call the rescue squad," said Troy. "I'm sorry Marion. It's my fault. I never should have encouraged you to play."

Minutes later the rescue wagon arrived and a competent team of medics quickly loaded Marion onto a stretcher and into the wagon and left for the emergency room.

Troy went over to Ava and said, "I'm going to go to the hospital. Can you keep Josh for me until I get back?"

"Sure. If it starts to rain, we'll go back to my place and you can come get him there, okay?"

"Thanks," said Troy. "I feel terrible. This is all my fault."

Ava reached out and grabbed Troy's arm as he turned away. "Hey," she said softly, "It's not your fault. These things happen. She'll be okay. Everything will be all right."

Troy looked at her bleakly. Then he managed a little smile. "Thanks. I wish you were right. But thanks for saying it anyway." Then he turned and left and Ava watched him walk away, wishing that she could have hugged him before he left. And then she stood there and puzzled over that feeling, and where it came from, and what it meant, until Josh tugged on her sleeve and said, "I guess the picnic's over now, huh?"

She looked down into his big gray eyes that looked just like Troy's, and felt dizzy for a minute before she pulled herself together and said, "Yeah. The picnic's over now."

To make matters even more perfect, the clouds rolled in shortly after the game broke up and by the time Ava and Josh were walking back to her apartment a light rain had begun to fall. Ava had apologized for not having recovered her car, but Josh didn't seem to mind walking. Even in the rain.

After they had walked for a couple of blocks during which they had discussed Josh's soccer team, his school, and his desire for a puppy, he looked point blank at Ava and said, "Do you like my dad?"

Ava swallowed. "Yeah. Yeah, I like your dad." She paused. "Why do you ask?"

Josh shifted the bag of soccer balls onto his other shoulder. "I was just wondering." He walked in silence for a few minutes. Then he said, "He doesn't have a girlfriend."

Ava concentrated on avoiding the puddles.

"Do you have a boyfriend?" Josh looked up at her.

Ava hesitated. She didn't want to be unkind. *But really. This isn't a Disney movie*, she thought. "I don't think we should talk about boyfriends or girlfriends, okay? Here's my building. We can watch TV or something till your dad gets here."

"Does he know where you live?"

Ava stopped on the top step. "Yeah. He knows. He gave me a ride home once."

"How come you don't have a car?"

"I have a car," said Ava, as they went in. "I just don't know where my keys are right now."

"Oh." Josh looked confused. He looked around at Ava's apartment, and Ava followed his glance taking in her spare minimalist décor. Josh observed, "It's cleaner than my dad's apartment."

"Really?" Ava didn't know what else to say. She led Josh to the couch in front of the television and handed him the remote. "Here. I'm sure you can find something to watch."

Ava went into her kitchen and put some water on to boil without really thinking. "Are you hungry?" she called out to Josh.

"No," he replied. Some kind of sitcom soundtrack came from the TV. Ava looked around the kitchen vaguely and realized she wasn't hungry either. She turned off the heat under the kettle and went out and sat down next to Josh. For several minutes they watched a rerun of "The Simpsons" without speaking. When the episode ended they looked at each other and Ava felt Josh studying her. She felt like she was being measured.

"Do you have a cat?" he asked.

"No. I don't have any pets."

"Why not? Don't you like animals?"

"No. I mean, yes, I like animals, I just don't have any right now."

"Did you have a dog when you were a kid?"

"No. My dad was in the military and we moved around a lot. So I never was allowed to have a pet."

Josh frowned. "Couldn't you take a pet with you when you moved?"

"I guess we could have. But my dad didn't think it was a good idea."

"Oh." Josh turned back to the TV and began flipping through the channels.

After another minute he said, "I thought you'd have a cat."

Ava raised her eyebrows. "Really? Well, I'm sorry. I don't. My friend does."

"What's her name?"

"My friend?"

"Yeah."

"Chenille. She's a teacher, like me."

"You're a teacher?" Josh turned to look at her gravely, as if she had just announced she had some contagious skin disease such as cooties.

Ava smiled at his reaction. "Yep."

Josh turned back to the TV. He tuned to "The Crocodile Hunter" and when the next ad came on he said, without turning around, "Why don't you have a cat?"

"I don't know. I guess I never thought about it. I'm not home very much because of my job and now the play. A cat would be alone all the time."

"Cats don't mind. My dad has a cat. They're not like dogs. Dogs like people. That's why I want a dog. A puppy."

"Yes. You told me."

"My mom doesn't understand," said Josh. "She thinks dogs are dirty and smelly. That's why I have to get my dad to let me move in with him, so I can get a dog."

Ava's eyes grew dark and she studied Josh's face, his delicate bones and determined expression. "I'm sure your dad would like to have you with him if he could," she said softly.

"Yeah. I know," Josh said, not looking up from the flickering screen.

Ava sat back on the couch and watched Josh without speaking for the next half hour until there was a light knock on the door. Ava opened it and Troy stood there, not looking much better than he had when he left.

"How is she?" asked Ava as Troy came in.

Josh turned off the television and came over and stood next to Ava, looking up at Troy. "Is she okay, Dad?"

Troy shook his head. "She's going to be okay. But her leg's broken and she's not going to be able to be in the play."

"Oh no!" said Ava, sinking down on the couch. Josh sat next to her and she put her arm around his slender shoulders without thinking. Troy looked at them together. Both of them were looking at him with the same expression. Troy almost smiled. Then he shifted his focus to Ava.

"Ava, I've been thinking about this ever since it happened, and I think there's only one thing we can do, and I don't know how you're going to feel about it, but maybe, it was the part you wanted all along, maybe it will turn out to be for the best. Although of course I feel terrible about Marion. She's in a lot of pain right now."

Ava felt a chill. "What do you mean?"

"Isn't it obvious?" said Troy. "Marion can't play Titania. The show opens in less than a week. You already know the part. I'm asking you to take over as Titania."

"Oh." Ava felt oddly flustered. She really hadn't been thinking about what would happen with the play at all. And she realized suddenly she couldn't remember when she must have stopped thinking about the role of Titania. In the last few weeks, since she began learning how to get laughs from the audience, enjoying the feeling of power it gave her, Ava had almost forgotten she had ever wanted any other part. And now she was being asked to change.

"Oh," she said again, flatly. She sucked her lower lip and stared at the rug. Maybe it would be nice to be Titania. She'd have to do scenes with Howard. *Ugh,* she thought. The hunk spell had worn off weeks ago. Now whenever she looked at Howard all she saw was his swollen ego and his shrunken sensitivity. He was the anti-Troy. Ava glanced up at Troy watching her, waiting for her reply. He was so selfless, so gentle. She knew if she said no he would find a way to get through it without her. But she realized that he was right. She already knew the part.

Still, she hesitated. She actually didn't look forward to the idea of giving up the power she'd found in playing Helena. "I don't know Troy. You know I didn't want the part of Helena, but now I think I'm getting the hang of it, and I kind of like getting laughs. I don't know if I should be Titania after all."

"I know, Ava. You've been getting better and better as Helena. You've been wonderful. And I'm sorry to have to ask you to change, but I don't think I have any choice. There's no one else who could just step right into the role. And you're the only one who's got a feel for the part, the regal bearing."

Ava laughed out loud. "Regal, huh?"

"You're a natural," Troy said, his eyes glowing with admiration.

Ava's breath quickened and she tightened her arm around Josh without thinking. He looked up at her curiously and she looked at him and said, "What do you think, Josh? Should I be the Queen of the Fairies?"

"Does that mean you'll be my boss?" he asked.

"Yeah. I guess it would."

Josh grinned. "Okay. Yeah. That would be cool."

Ava shrugged at Troy. "Well, okay then. I guess I can't say no."

Troy's face relaxed for the first time since he'd walked in and he said, "Thanks, Ava. I'll make it up to you."

"Hey, you made me a queen. That's enough," she smiled.

"Right." Troy sank onto a chair as if the weight of the day had finally settled on him and Ava suddenly realized that he probably hadn't eaten in hours.

"Are you hungry?" she asked. "Can I fix you anything? Or would you guys like to order a pizza?"

"Pizza!" crowed Josh happily.

"The magic word," said Troy.

"Well, I am Queen of the Fairies, after all," said Ava, going to the phone.

Chapter Eight

"**I**'m a real girl! I'm a real girl!"

Bouncing with delight after being promoted from fairy-hood to the role of Helena, Iris went scampering around the theatre like Pinocchio after his transformation. After briefly considering the possibilities Troy had chosen the giddy Goth fairy because he felt she could slip into the role effectively, and with her dark spiky hair and slight air of menace, she could provide effective balance for Heather's unrelenting perkiness.

Heather welcomed the change, figuring she could probably take Iris in a fight, if it came to that, and after the weeks of buffeting from Ava, Heather wasn't taking anything for granted. Jason and Brad also seemed relieved to have one of their peers in the role, though Iris warned them she was still a fairy at heart.

Watching the first rehearsal after the cast change, Troy felt his nerves settling. This was so right. The pieces fit perfectly, especially when Iris mimicked Ava's slapstick moves. But when Ava first stepped on the stage as Titania, Troy felt the back of his neck prickle with excitement. She seemed a different person than when she'd read for the part months ago at auditions. Now, she was sure and vibrant. The light shimmered about her and her dark eyes flashed with erotic power. Troy shifted uncomfortably in his seat, glad he was sitting down in the dark.

Howard had all but cheered when the news of Marion's departure from the cast was announced, and he promptly turned his practiced leer upon Ava. Finding her alone backstage before the rehearsal he leaned against her and muttered huskily, "So, my queen, you'll have to come to my dressing room for some private rehearsals."

"In your dreams," snapped Ava, twisting out from under Howard's arm.

"Ooh, I like 'em feisty," he said.

Ava shuddered with distaste, nearly choking on the vapor barrier of Howard's cologne. She stood in the wings and wrestled with her own wistful feelings as she watched Iris stepping into the role of Helena. Ava was happy for the Goth sprite, and touched to see that Iris was playing the character with a lot of spunk and flair.

But, when it came time for her to make her first entrance as Titania, Ava found she had no regrets. She felt as if she'd earned the title. In the opening verbal sparring match with Oberon, Ava used her body to underscore the dialogue, and when she glanced out at Troy following the scene she could see the light of approval shining in his eyes.

The rehearsal ran way late Monday, and Ava didn't get home until almost 1 A.M. Troy had promised he wouldn't keep them so long the next night, but Ava doubted he could really control the time anymore. There was still so much to do, and opening night just four nights away.

All day Tuesday Ava dragged herself through her classes, trying not to talk, saving her energy for the long night ahead. When she got to the theatre Nina was on the stage, ordering changes in the lighting. Tech aides were adjusting the sound system and the costumer was fitting the large donkey head on Bottom for the first time. Tim Murphy, the veteran playing the boastful weaver, was staggering around on center stage, trying to get accustomed to the awkward weight on his shoulders.

"Awhm nawg ar aydu zee undis," he said, his voice muffled by the donkey fur.

"What?" said the costumer.

Nina turned and frowned. "That's not going to work," she said. "I can't understand a word he's saying. And you can hardly hear him."

Tim wrenched the head off and held it in front of his red face. "I can't see a thing in this. The eye holes have got to be bigger."

The costumer nodded. "Okay. Give it to me. I'll work on it some more."

Looking for the source of an irregular "thunk, thunk" sound coming from the foot of the stage, Ava saw Josh and Alex kicking a soccer ball against the edge of the orchestra pit. She noticed they were avoiding a wet towel spread a few feet from the steps to the stage.

"I see you've noticed our leak," said Troy, coming up beside her.

"Gosh. That's not great is it?"

"Nope. But there's not much we can do about it. Let's just hope the rain stops soon."

Ava glanced around, taking in the banging, thunking, clattering, and general chaos, "Is it always this bad during Hell Week?"

"Pretty much," said Troy. "Don't worry. It'll all come together by opening night."

Ava looked doubtfully at the stage, where Theseus and Egeus stood patiently framed by a pair of plaster classical columns. Nearby Nigel sat on the floor doing card tricks for a couple of admiring fairy girls. The smell of microwave popcorn drifted down from the lobby, mixing with the scent of paint and sweat from backstage.

"I don't know how you can be so calm," said Ava. Troy looked up from his clipboard full of notes and smiled.

"I'm not really calm. I just have to pretend to be so that everyone else doesn't panic."

"Oh." Ava let her eyes linger on Troy. He was wearing his usual blue work shirt, a pair of faded jeans and well-worn Timberlands. While she was still staring at him he turned to look at her and their eyes met. He smiled and Ava couldn't help smiling back and he said, "Hey. You were really great last night. I'm sorry Marion got hurt, but having you in the part is fantastic. There's a kind of chemistry between you and Howard that works better. There was too much real friction between him and Marion and I think it got in the way of their performance together."

"Oh. Thanks." Ava looked away for a minute. "You know, there's friction between Howard and me too."

"Yeah. I know. But it doesn't show in your performance, and that's what matters."

"Well, thanks. I'll try to keep it that way."

Later, when Ava was going through the scenes with Howard, she noticed the edge in his voice and the heat in his eyes and she was startled to realize that the fairy king definitely seemed turned on, and she didn't think it was just part of his act. *Great,* she thought. *Now that I've decided he's a twerp, he finds me attractive.*

At the end of the night Ava saw Howard heading toward her. She quickly attached herself to a group of fairies and mechanicals, cadging a ride to avoid the rainy walk home and Howard's unwelcome advances.

The next day Chenille stopped into Ava's office and asked if she could come to rehearsal that night.

"Sure, but I warn you, it's really crazy right now. Everyone's getting crabby because there's so little time left and people are still making mistakes and the costumes aren't finished, even though we're supposed to be having dress rehearsal tonight, and you know, we changed the cast." Ava smiled as she said this last part and Chenille laughed.

"Well, duh! Why do you think I want to come? Last time I

saw you do your Helena thing. But I want to see how you mix it up with Hunkeron."

Ava sniffed dismissively.

"What?" Chenille tilted her head to one side. "Is there something I should know?"

Ava shrugged. She tapped a pencil on her desk and began to doodle loopy circles around the word May on her calendar. "No." She looked out the window where the tulip poplar was beginning to unfurl its green flags.

"It's just that I'm not attracted to Howard anymore."

"Really! Does that mean he's up for grabs?" Chenille's big blue eyes opened wider.

Ava spun her chair around facing Chenille. "Let's just put it this way. If there's grabbing to be done, Howard will do it."

Chenille frowned. "You mean he went for you and you turned him down?"

"More or less."

"Wow. So what's wrong with him? Is he a creep in hunk's clothing?"

"Kind of. Only, I guess he's not really a creep. He's just . . . not very special. You know? Like he looks like he should be so great, and he's like one of those chocolate cakes that looks fantastic and then you bite into it and it's kind of dry and tasteless?"

"I wouldn't mind trying a bite of old Howard. If you're not interested."

"Be my guest. He's not a bad guy. Maybe you could bring out the best in him, Nille. Maybe you're the woman who can turn the toad into a prince."

"That's frogs, isn't it?"

"Close enough."

Chenille smiled. "All righty. Count me in."

As Chenille stood to go, Ava said, "Oh, if you're coming tonight, could you give me a ride?"

"You still haven't gotten your car back? They're going to tow it away if you leave it there too long you know."

"Yeah. I know. Really, this weekend, I'm going to find my spare keys."

Chenille smiled and shook her head. "Pick you up at six forty-five?"

"Thanks."

As Ava slipped into the feather light costume she reflected that at least it was a step up from the shapeless sheet she would have had to wear as Helena. Titania's diaphanous gown was moss green and violet, light as a butterfly's wing and just as enchanting. Wearing it, Ava felt curiously empowered. The unmistakable ogling from the men in the show when she first appeared in the dress enhanced this sensation.

When Troy looked up and saw her in the costume he stared without speaking for half a second, then said, "Wow" softly.

Seeing Chenille out in the audience Ava twirled for her and smiled happily.

"It looks better on you than it did on Marion," said Iris, coming out in her white shift.

"Oh. Thanks. I feel so bad for Marion, but I love getting to wear this costume. It feels like I have nothing on at all."

"Really?" said Howard, emerging from the wing. "That I'd like to see."

"Don't hold your breath," said Ava, losing her smile.

"Places everyone," called Troy. With only two nights left till opening night, this rehearsal was supposed to run just like a regular performance, beginning and ending on time, with no stops for corrections. If all went according to plan.

By midway through the second act it was clear that they would not end at the target time, and, as the performance wore on, and the delays mounted, Troy found it impossible to keep the frustration out of his voice.

It was nearly midnight by the time he finished giving notes and as Ava walked out with Chenille she said, "I'm really sorry you had to sit through all of that. It hasn't been this bad before. I guess Troy's starting to freak out that we're really going to stink on opening night."

Chenille grabbed Ava's hand and said, "Hey, I understand. I think you all are doing great. And I don't blame Troy for being nervous. It means a lot to him. You can tell." She looked at Ava with a little smirk.

Ava slumped against the seat in Chenille's car and considered ignoring the smirk. She had an idea what was behind it. But then she decided it wasn't fair to deny Chenille the fun of delivering her post-rehearsal analysis.

"Okay. What did you think of the way it's going?" said Ava, folding her arms across her chest with a resigned sigh.

"Well, since you ask, I think it's much better having you as Titania, even though I kind of missed watching you rough-up Demetrius. And most of the play seems to be in good shape. I think it drags a little at the start. To tell you the truth, tonight I kept getting distracted watching Troy watch Howard, so I wasn't paying as close attention to the play as I might have."

Ava studied Chenille's face. "What do you mean?"

Chenille shrugged slightly. "I thought I was imagining it at first, but, well . . ."

"What?"

Chenille parked the car in front of Ava's building and said, "Every time Howard oozes close to you, every time he mentions your name, his face gets this kind of creepy expression, and Troy was glaring at him the whole time. Like he was jealous or something. When, really, I think Oberon is supposed to be kind of a creep—you know? I mean what kind of a guy would drug his wife to make her fall for a donkey? So, there's Howard playing his part, right? But Troy is not looking at all happy about it, and when he gave his notes later, he didn't say anything at all to Howard. Doesn't that seem odd?"

Chenille looked so pleased with herself, and Ava was so worn out that she didn't bother to argue. Let Chenille think whatever she wanted. *Just let me go to sleep now*, thought Ava. "Hmm. That's an interesting theory, Nille. I'll sleep on it, okay?" Ava got out of the car.

"Okay. But hey, I can't give you a ride tomorrow. Find those keys."

Ava nodded sleepily. "Right. Tomorrow."

In the empty theatre Troy sat listening to the drip from the leaking roof, which had increased to the point that a bucket marked the spot. Troy felt like he did every night after rehearsal, drained of physical energy, but too emotionally wound up to rest. He knew he should go home. He needed to sleep.

This business of working all day and directing all night was eating away at his sanity. That's what he told himself anyway. What other reason could there be for the feverish way he felt? Every time he saw Ava across the stage his pulse skipped and he lost his place in the script. And he was beginning to worry that somebody would notice. Tonight there had been that friend of Ava's, the blonde. Troy could feel her eyes watching him and he tried extra hard to keep his emotions hidden. But he couldn't help it. And it made him sick to listen to that goon Howard with his smarmy innuendo and his constant leer. Troy wished he could switch him to another part, but that was out of the question.

Troy leaned back and closed his eyes and thought of the way Ava had looked in that slinky costume. Maybe it just looked better on her because she was so tall, so elegant. Troy thought she looked sensational.

He knew, though, that Ava considered her height a problem. She was so oversensitive about it. Troy imagined that it must have been difficult for her as a young girl, when she first began to tower over the boys. Troy knew from personal experience how rigid the traditional view was, the idea that the boy should be taller than the girl. He could still vividly recall the humiliating experiences of middle school dances, being turned down by girls who were taller than him when he asked them to dance. But, Troy had never been bothered about his height. Until he realized that it might keep him from having a chance with Ava. He wondered just how much it bothered her.

Troy couldn't stop thinking about her. The way her voice caressed the lines. She really had a fantastic voice. It was funny, Troy mused, thinking back to his first sight of Ava. He hadn't noticed anything out of the ordinary. Well, maybe that smile. And her nose. It wasn't one of those cute turned up things like Kerry had. It was long and thin and maybe even some people would say it was too big. But on Ava's face it was wonderful, like Sophia Loren or something. Troy sighed. In two weeks the play would be over. And Ava Morrison would probably disappear from his life.

Troy sat up and shook himself. Mustn't allow himself to get down. He wasn't ready for a relationship anyway. Not until Josh was older, at least. Troy flashed on how Ava had looked with her arm around Josh in her apartment. The image lingered in his mind's eye until he shook himself and stood up. *Don't kid yourself*, he thought. *She thinks you're too short.*

He gathered his things and started toward the exit. As he did so he noticed with dismay a new puddle in the aisle. If only the rain would at least stop.

Chapter Nine

The drilling rain woke Ava at dawn when she sat up in bed and thought, *This is a sign. I am finding those keys now.*

It took her forty-five minutes of opening drawers, searching cabinets, and checking pockets in every jacket in her closet, but the spare set finally clinked at her from a coffee cup on the seldom used top shelf in her kitchen where she finally remembered having carefully put them so she wouldn't lose them.

Her sense of triumph was short-lived, however, when she suddenly remembered that though she now had the keys, her car was still sitting in the lot at the park, a long and wet walk away. As she finished getting ready for class she resolved that she would pick up the car after work and drive herself to the final dress rehearsal that night.

The rain continued without mercy all day long, and when Ava got out of her last class she opened her umbrella and set out with the wind whipping the rain sideways. By the time she'd trudged the twelve blocks to the park she was drenched. At least her car was still there, though a pink paper fluttering on the windshield looked suspiciously like a ticket.

"Perfect," said Ava reading the citation for abandoning her vehicle. She brightened when the car started right up. In the last few damp blocks troubling doubts about the car battery had nagged her. She drove home, changed into some dry clothes, grabbed a quick dinner, and headed to the theatre, feeling in a good mood to be back in the driver's seat with just one more night till the play opened.

Ava was so focused on finding a close parking space that she didn't notice the crowd of umbrellas in front of the theatre until she was almost on top of them. She tried to see past them and caught a glimpse of yellow ribbon, the kind of caution tape that cops put around accidents.

"What's going on?" she asked as she stepped next to Iris and Alex, sharing a big black and yellow VCU umbrella.

They turned stricken faces on her and said, in unison, "The roof caved in."

"What!" Ava looked around at the grave faces of other cast members. She didn't see Troy. "Where's Troy? Was anyone inside? Was anyone hurt?"

Nina edged next to her and said, "No one was inside, thank God. It must have happened after we left last night, because Troy was the first to arrive this afternoon and he says it was already ruined."

"Ruined?"

Nina grimaced. "Everything. The sets, the props. The costumes are okay. The dressing rooms only caved in halfway because they're against the back wall. But the theatre is . . ." Nina shook her head.

A silent pall hung beneath the canopy of wet umbrellas while the rain continued to patter. After a moment Ava asked, "Is Troy inside?"

"Yes," said Nina. "He's in there with the cops and the insurance agent."

"Does this mean we have to cancel the play?"

Nina frowned. She inhaled deeply and looked around at the cast members who were all waiting for her answer. Finally she said, "Well, folks, they always say the show must go on. But we're going to have to work a miracle here. If anybody has any brilliant ideas, I'm ready to listen."

Rain skittered off the umbrellas while no one said a word.

After a few minutes Nina said, "You may as well all go home now. We'll call everyone in the morning to let you know what we're going to do."

Ava hung around for a few minutes longer, feeling helpless and worried. She hadn't really accepted the idea that the play wasn't going to happen. She just kept thinking about Troy, and how crushed he must be feeling. She wanted to see him, to reassure him that somehow they'd find a way. But, standing there in the dark rain, Ava had to admit that at the moment she didn't have any particularly brilliant ideas.

After a few more minutes she noticed Nina was still standing under the marquee, explaining the situation to late arrivals. Ava went over to her and said, "I guess I'm gonna head home. Tell Troy to call me if . . ." she hesitated, unsure how to finish the sentence. She wanted to talk to Troy. She didn't know why.

Nina was looking at her curiously. "If . . . ?" she prompted.

Ava shrugged. "I don't know. Just tell him he can call me if he wants to talk."

"Okay," said Nina, studying Ava's face. "We'll figure something out. Don't worry."

"Okay. I hope you're right," said Ava, and walked back to her car.

As soon as she got home she called Chenille and told her the news.

"Oh my God! That's terrible!" Chenille responded with all the sympathy Ava could have expected, but she didn't have any miraculous suggestions for where they could stage the play.

As she was getting ready to hang up, Ava mumbled, "It's too bad we can't just do it outside somewhere."

Chenille gasped.

"Are you okay, Nille? You sound like you just choked on something."

"That's it!" squeaked Chenille. "Outside! You could put the play on under the trees and it would be like a living set!"

Ava began pacing back and forth with the cordless phone, thinking about possible sites. "Maybe," she muttered. "Of course the rain kind of . . ."

"That's what makes this so perfect!" squealed Chenille. "I was just watching the evening news and Chaz the weather guy says the rains are absolutely stopping tomorrow. He gave it one of his scout's honor guarantees."

"Really? And that's binding on God, is it?"

"Oh come on, Ave. You gotta have faith. This could be fantastic. Better even than that moldy old theatre."

Ava sat down, thinking hard. "But where, Nille? Where is there an amphitheater we could use? And we can't really pay for some place. At least I don't think we could. Not now."

A silence stretched between them for almost a minute. Then Ava spoke. "Are you still there?"

"Yeah. I'm thinking."

"Me too. How about Maymont? Don't they have a space that would work?"

"Wow! That would be perfect! And I bet they'd be happy to let you guys do it there too, for maybe some portion of the ticket sales or something."

Ava started pacing again, picking up speed. She wanted to find Troy and tell him her idea immediately. She wanted to see him smile.

"Nille, I'm going to call Troy."

"Great. Let me know as soon as you get something settled. I can help you spread the word to the radio stations and stuff."

"Okay. I hadn't thought of that."

"Yeah. If they go for it, it's still going to take a lot of work to pull it off."

"Right. I'll talk to you soon. Thanks Nille."

After Ava hung up she found Troy's number and called, but his machine answered and she didn't want to leave a long message, so she just left her number. She looked around her apartment and couldn't stand the idea of waiting for the phone to ring. She grabbed her purse and headed back to the theatre.

After the insurance agent and the news people left and the cops had finished documenting the scene, Troy was left alone in the dark, wet theatre. The rain was letting up, but a cool drizzle was still streaming through the yawning opening where the roof had collapsed. Large chunks of plaster and shingle covered most of the center seats in the theatre. With the occasional shaft of blue light pulsing through from the police cars still parked outside, the place reminded Troy of a setting in *Bladerunner,* full of dank post-industrial decay.

Troy felt numb. He had worked so hard. Those sets had taken weeks to get just right. And now, even if he could beg a place for a stage, to let the actors at least perform, it wouldn't be, it couldn't be the same.

Nina had told him to go home and sleep on it. "Maybe you'll dream up a solution," she'd suggested, half-seriously.

But, exhausted though he was, Troy didn't feel like sleeping. He felt like he'd been mugged.

"Troy? Troy are you still here?"

Ava's voice wavered in the darkness like a torchlight. Troy turned toward her, his heart beating faster, and for once, he ignored his rational mind's cautionary advice.

"Ava?" he said, even though he knew her voice, her amazing voice. He just wanted to hear it again.

"I tried your phone, but when I realized you weren't home I thought you might still be here and I wanted to talk to you right away."

The urgency in her voice thrilled Troy. She was coming down the aisle, wearing a hooded rain parka, holding a dripping umbrella. Her hair was damp and her skin was pale but there was a light of excitement in her eyes and Troy felt it like an electrical charge.

"I have an idea," she said eagerly. Ava looked at Troy and he stared back at her, his gray eyes darker in the half-light. She couldn't read him.

"I was talking to Chenille about what we could do, and I remembered Maymont! We could put on the show on the grounds of Maymont I'll bet. They would probably be glad to let us if we gave them a portion of the ticket sales. What do you think?" Ava smiled hopefully at Troy.

He continued to stare at her without speaking for another minute, and Ava was just beginning to wonder if maybe he was in shock or something or maybe he needed medical treatment, when he said quietly, "You are amazing."

He shook his head as if in disbelief. "That's a great idea. I think that could work." He sat down on the edge of one of the theatre seats, and Ava noticed then that every surface in the theatre was soaking wet. She looked up and saw rain clouds thinning in the night sky through the gaping hole where the roof used to be. It looked like a moon was trying to peek through.

Troy followed her gaze and saw the moon.

" 'Ill met by moonlight proud Titania,' " he said softly.

Ava smiled. "It could work though don't you think?"

A small smile worked its way across Troy's wet face. He nodded. "Yes. I think it could work. It might even be incredible. Thank you, Ava." He paused. He swallowed and seemed to be considering saying something more. Ava felt again the nearly overpowering urge to wrap her arms around him and tell him everything would be all right. But she wasn't sure if he would appreciate that. He might think she was patronizing him. *Hah! There's a switch*, she thought.

Troy stood up, and Ava felt a twinge of bitterness as she saw his eyes were not quite level with hers, but she smiled at him anyway and when he put his arms around her and hugged her she felt her heart race and her cheeks flushed.

"You've been wonderful all through this, with Marion, and Howard, and Nigel, and now this. I don't know what I would have done without you."

Ava struggled to think of something to say. All she could manage was, "You don't have to thank me. I'm so glad you gave me a part. And . . . I've . . . really . . . learned a lot working with you," she finished lamely. It wasn't what she wanted to say, but suddenly, after that hug, she didn't know how to put into words what she was feeling.

Luckily, Troy was energized by the new idea, and he grabbed her hand and started leading her up the aisle as he said, "I've got to find Nina and get her started on Maymont right away. Maybe she could call one of the park administrators tonight. Our story is going to be on the late news. We've got to move fast."

He stopped for a second and faced Ava again. "And I owe it all to you." He kissed her quickly on the cheek and bounded up the rest of the aisle and Ava stood there watching him leave, her pulse percolating with a charge that had nothing to do with espresso.

Her phone began ringing at 7 A.M. the next morning. First Troy, pumped and playful. She'd never heard him sound so fired up, and even before she'd had her first cup of coffee she found his enthusiasm wildly contagious.

Minutes after he hung up Chenille checked in, ecstatic about the new plan. She volunteered to help get the word out on campus, and to come early to Maymont to help with details. Troy had told Ava that Nina would take care of all their logistics, moving the lights, arranging a curtained temporary backstage where they could get into their costumes, and figuring out how to arrange the seating. But Ava imagined that the job would be too big for one woman, even one as organized as Nina.

Then to Ava's surprise, Iris called, wanting a ride to Maymont later. Ava gladly agreed. "We Helenas should stick together," she told Iris.

Ava struggled to stay focused during her two classes, and beat her students to the exit when 3:00 finally arrived. She was heartened to see flyers announcing the play posted in the halls as she left the building. *Pretty quick work, Nille,* she thought.

Arriving at Maymont, Ava and Iris weren't sure where to park, but a volunteer helped them find a good spot, and then directed them to the clearing at the foot of a gentle slope where the play would be staged.

"Oh," said Iris. "I thought we would be up in the Italian garden."

"Too formal," barked Nina, glancing up from overseeing the positioning of a light tower. "Most of the action takes place in the magical forest. It would be nice if we could do the opening and closing scenes in the Italian garden, but I don't think we can ask the audience to follow us around. And we can't light up the whole park."

"This will be great," said Ava.

A makeshift curtain stretched between two massive oaks. Two groups of folding chairs were arranged in rows at the base of the gentle hillside where more audience members could sit on the grass.

Ava looked for Troy but didn't see him out front. "Let's go find the dressing rooms, if we have any," she said to Iris.

They found Troy deep in consultation with a couple of students setting up a sound board. Troy looked up as they approached and said, "It's going to be tricky with the sound out here."

A young man with earphones wrapped around his neck and a ring in his eyebrow met Ava's inquiring gaze and said, "I can't turn it up very loud out here or we're going to have bad feedback, because of the way the hill bounces the sound. I'll give you as much as I can, but you guys are going to have to project."

Ava saw Troy watching her, waiting for her reaction.

"Okay," she said, smoothly. "We can do that." *I hope*, she thought, as she and Iris walked away.

The next few hours passed quickly as the cast and crew worked together to solve the new set of problems created by moving the show outside. But, Ava noted gratefully, at least the rain had stayed away. And as the sun began to set just before 8:00, she could see the moon beginning its ascent behind the trees. *What could be more perfect?* she thought.

The actors gathered behind the trees and the curtain billowing gently in the evening breeze. From out front they could hear the growing murmur of the crowd.

"Well, I'd say we had a full house, if we were in a house," announced Nina quietly.

Troy stepped forward and said, "Okay gang. I'm going to go out and introduce our play. No matter what happens after this moment, I just want you to know that being here tonight with all of you is . . ." he inhaled deeply and looked up at the moon for a second.

"Insane?" offered Nigel.

Troy smiled. "I was going to say wonderful but maybe you're right. Anyway. Thanks. To everyone. I've never had so much fun losing my mind. Now I want you to go out there and make the audience lose theirs."

Some of the cast did a wordless high five, and Troy slipped in front of the curtain. They heard him say a few words, then the taped music began and they started the show.

The first few minutes seemed to crawl for Ava waiting backstage. The utter silence from the audience was chilling. Then, after a small eternity, Hermia spoke her first lines, and even from the muffled backstage perspective Ava could hear Heather's valley girl inflections and the whisper of appreciation from the audience. But, things really picked up when Iris stalked on stage. Her punk rock Helena injected a welcome jolt of emotion into the first scene and peeking out at the audience, Ava could see that they were paying attention now.

And that could have been me, she thought wistfully. But, her regret was fleeting. In all honesty, Ava was excited about assuming the role of Titania. And she was happy for Iris, who had literally blossomed into Helena. A surge of happiness flowed through Ava and at that moment she saw Troy at the opposite end of the backstage area. He was watching the action on stage, his face serious but calm. Ava stared at him without thinking for several minutes until Nigel nudged her elbow and said, "Nervous?"

Ava jumped slightly. Then frowned seeing it was Nigel. "No. Just thinking. You should try it sometime."

"Huh," snorted Nigel and moved off. Ava shivered with distaste.

Since Titania's entry didn't come until the second act, Ava had plenty of time to prepare herself mentally for her first public performance, but as the seconds sped by, she felt her heart thudding faster. No turning back now.

Then, suddenly, it was time to go on. She walked in front of the curtain and the lights hit her and she felt the world shift. There was Howard, looking stern and potent, an angry Oberon impatient with his queen. Ava responded in character and the sparks flew between them. When the second act closed the audience applauded loudly and the energy level backstage rose accordingly.

From that point on, the show soared. Everyone got laughs. The rude mechanicals surpassed themselves and people in the audience chuckled loudly. The big fight scene between Hermia and Helena took the slapstick up another notch, and the audience howled.

It all happened so quickly. Suddenly Ava was out on the grass, taking her bow for the curtain call, and she felt happy, but also like her engine was racing and she had nowhere to go. Clutching the bouquet of lavender roses that Nina had given her during the ovation, Ava accepted compliments and congratulations from Chenille and some of the other faculty members and students who had come. As the crowd began to disperse, Tim Murphy handed Ava a flyer.

"Directions to my house," he said.

Ava looked at the paper, an invitation to the first cast party beginning as soon as everyone got to the Murphys' home, just on the other side of the river.

"Ava, fairy queen, will you give us a ride?" asked Iris, with an arm around Alex.

"Sure, you can help me find the place," said Ava.

Half an hour later they were drinking champagne on the deck of the Murphys' suburban colonial. Jane Murphy had strung tiny Christmas lights all around the deck perimeter. Large jars filled with fragrant lilac competed with the cigarettes. From somewhere inside a CD of The Strokes played.

"I didn't know you were a Strokes fan," said Iris, as Tim showed them to the deck.

"It's my daughter's. When I told her we were having the cast party here she insisted on being the DJ."

"Cool," said Iris.

Tim rolled his eyes at Ava.

The champagne tasted so good, and Ava was so thirsty, she gulped down the first glass like it was ginger ale and quickly got a refill. The second she sipped more slowly, looking around for Troy. He was at the far side of the deck, standing next to Howard and Tim, both of whom loomed over him. Ava couldn't take her eyes off Troy.

His face was flushed and his hair was messed up. He was laughing and talking with the other two, but while they guffawed and flung their arms about as they talked, Troy sipped his drink looking mildly amused. He was leaning with his hip against the deck rail, his thumb hooked inside his jean pocket, the other hand holding a beer. He looked so relaxed. Ava was still staring at him when he glanced in her direction and his dark eyes locked onto hers and she felt it like a blow to the chest.

She kept staring as he detached himself from the other two men and walked toward her, never taking his eyes off her. When he got closer, he said in a husky voice, "There's something I've been wanting to do all night."

He grabbed Ava's hand and pulled her gently but firmly to the stairs leading off the deck. She followed him to the lawn where he turned around and faced her. Then he got a funny look on his face, and Ava began to wonder if he was just playing a joke, but he stepped behind her onto the bottom step of the deck stairs, then he turned to face her and she tried not to smile as she realized that, from this angle, he was exactly as tall as she was.

"Okay," he said. "This may be cheating, but I don't care." And he pulled her closer and kissed her firmly. His lips were warm and tasted sweet and Ava relaxed into the kiss, feeling his hands in her hair, and his body close against hers.

When he pulled away Ava saw the dark fire in his eyes and she leaned into the next kiss, wanting him. His hands moved down her back and pulled her against him and she pushed into him, feeling hot and hungry.

For several minutes they got lost in each other. Then Ava heard someone calling Troy's name from above. She let go of him and he held her for a moment longer before he said, without looking around, "What?"

"Troy, are you down there? Josh has been looking for you. He said something about a game tomorrow?" It was Nina, tactfully staying up on the deck.

Troy sighed. "Okay. Tell him I'll be right there," he called. Then he said softly to Ava. "I have to go. He's got a game tomorrow morning, early."

Ava smiled. "I understand," she said.

"You could come watch. It's at eight at Byrd Park."

"Ouch."

"It's okay. I don't expect to see you there." Troy smiled and looked at her for another minute.

"So, I guess you'd better be going, huh?" she said.

"Yeah, I guess so," he said, still with his arms around her. He leaned closer and kissed her once more, softly. Then he whispered, "I'll see you tomorrow night."

"Okay," she replied, wondering if he was going to make other plans for Josh tomorrow.

Troy left and Ava stood there in the moonlight wondering what had just happened, and if she was glad about it, and if she should be. She went back to the party. But, after another half hour of talking with everyone but Troy, Ava felt exhausted. She looked around for a reason to stay longer, but couldn't see one. She found Iris and Alex and asked if they wanted a ride back to campus. Alex, who was drinking Dr. Pepper, looked at her oddly and said, "Let me drive you home, Ava."

Ava frowned, weaving just a little, but decided she was too tired to argue. Later, when she was collapsing onto her bed, Ava thought about Troy standing on the step so he could get better leverage for kissing her, and she laughed out loud. She was still smiling when she fell asleep moments later.

Chapter Ten

Ava woke with a pounding head to the sound of someone knocking at her door. This was a rare enough sound to lure her out of the warm cocoon of her bed. She shuffled to the door and peeked through the view hole to see Chenille quivering in the dark hallway. She opened the door and Chenille burst in waving a newspaper.

"Have you seen it yet?" she asked.

Ava pushed her hair off her face and said, "No. I was still in bed."

"Oh right. Late night and all. I'm sorry. I just got so excited when I read it that I had to see you. It's so great!"

Ava tried to follow Chenille's bouncing movement around the living room but it hurt her head to turn that quickly, so she sat down on the couch and said quietly, "What is so great?"

Chenille stopped in mid-bounce and looked at Ava wide-eyed. "The review! The critic from the *Dispatch* came last night and he loved it! He said you were especially good. And he mentioned Iris too. And he said nice things about Troy and how effective it was being outside and all. It's a really great review. I bet you guys get a much bigger audience because of it."

Chenille plopped on the couch next to Ava and watched as Ava read the review. It was true. The reviewer loved the show. He called the cast "nimble" and "spirited" and he praised Troy for his "intelligent and highly entertaining" direction.

Ava sat back and almost forgot her headache. The reviewer had singled her out for her "beautiful elocution" and "graceful movement." Ava closed her eyes and basked in the praise. She'd have to send a copy to her parents. *Hah. It's never too late to get the last word,* she thought.

Chenille was beaming at her. "So, can I take you out for lunch? Or brunch as the case may be? Now that you're a star, I want to be seen with you. Maybe it will help my chances with Howard."

Ava winced. "Oh Nille, you're too good for him. He's an oaf, you know."

"Yeah, I know. But he's my kind of oaf. Tall, dark, and over-sexed. Guys like that just need the right woman to whip them into shape. I've been watching Wowie-Howie and I think I can take him."

Ava grinned and shook her head, instantly regretting the movement which unleashed a firestorm of pain at her temples. She winced and said, "Okay, have it your way. But don't say I didn't warn you."

"Hey, just prepare yourself to wear pink," said Chenille.

"Pink?"

"All my bridesmaids will be in pink," explained Chenille, smiling sweetly.

Chenille's prediction turned out to be on the money. When Ava arrived at 7:00 she was greeted by a pair of giddy Maymont staffers who said they had already sold more tickets for tonight's performance than they had the night before. As Ava neared the stage area she could see picnic blankets checkerboarding the sloping hill, where clusters of people were eating and drinking al fresco before the show.

When she went behind the curtain to begin getting into her costume she saw Troy deep in conversation with Nigel. Nigel's face was red and he looked unhappy about something. Ava tried to imagine what that could be. She couldn't remember the reviewer saying anything negative about Puck. But, then, now that she thought about it, the reviewer hadn't said anything at all about Puck. Maybe Nigel was upset about that? Whatever it was, he was wound up.

Ava was just about to go into the small tent set up for the women's dressing room when she noticed Josh kicking a soccer ball back and forth with Alex. "Hey Josh. Did your team win this morning?" she asked.

Josh trapped the ball with his foot before looking over. His face lit up when he saw her. "Five-nil!" he said. "And I had a hat trick!"

"Great," said Ava, wondering what a hat trick was. Something good, obviously.

A half hour later darkness was beginning to thicken under the trees when Ava finished getting ready and stepped out of the tent. She saw the fairies blowing bubbles at the edge of the curtain, where the air carried them up and out over the audience. She looked for Troy and noticed him talking earnestly with Nina. She wondered if he would try to speak with her before the show or after. While she watched, Heather came up to him, escorting a radiant blonde woman, who might be her mother. *Or maybe her sister,* thought Ava, on closer examination of the woman's dewy skin and voluptuous figure. She watched as Heather introduced the woman, who was gushing all over Troy and he didn't seem to mind, Ava noticed.

Her good mood somewhat deflated, Ava turned away to find Iris and saw instead Howard, flirting clumsily with one of the other fairies, a little redhead who had no lines in the play but seemed to enjoy wearing tulle wings anyway. The redhead laughed and rolled her eyes at Howard, but quickly escaped and for a minute Ava saw Howard standing alone, a man rejected, and for just a moment Ava thought she saw a shadow of weariness, maybe even loneliness, cross his handsome features. Hmmph, thought Ava. Maybe Chenille could make something of him after all.

When she turned back to see if Troy was through with Heather's blonde friend, Ava couldn't see him anywhere. It was getting late, almost time to start.

Someone thumped her on the shoulder and Ava turned and saw Troy jogging to the other side of the curtain. He glanced back over his shoulder as he went by and said, "Break a leg, Ava."

Ava felt like she'd been slapped. She saw Troy step out in front of the curtain and give his little speech. She listened numbly, thoughts swirling in her head. She had been expecting something else. What? Tenderness? Embarrassment? Some weak attempt at humor maybe? Not a casual punch on the shoulder, as if she were some soccer teammate. He'd kissed her. Was that just the excitement talking?

Ava tried to tell herself she was overreacting. He was busy. He had to focus on the show. Right. She should focus on the show. Right.

But even as she forced herself to act like nothing was wrong, Ava felt a chill and she didn't know why.

The performance went well. Everyone was "nimble" and "spirited" and Ava had a moment of bliss when the audience burst into applause after she made her first speech. And they howled with laughter when she and Tim played the famous "love" scene while he was wearing his donkey head. But, when the curtain call arrived, Ava went through the motions without quite the same carefree joy she'd felt the night before.

And tonight there was no cast party. Knowing they had to return early on Sunday for the matinee performance the cast had voted to make an early night of it. Only a few of the fairies and the younger techies were going bar-hopping after the show. But not until Ava caught sight of Troy whisking

Josh off to his truck without saying even goodnight did she give in to the feeling of disappointment that had plagued her all night.

He's sorry he kissed me, she thought. *That's why he's avoiding me. What an idiot I am. He wants to forget it happened. Okay. I can do that.*

But as she drove home to her quiet, empty apartment, Ava was haunted by the memory of how happy she'd been for those few moments in the moonlight.

Troy tucked Josh in and turned out the light. He went into the kitchen and opened the refrigerator, got a beer and took it out to the dark living room. He sat on the couch, felt for the remote, clicked on the tube and sat there in the dark drinking and watching David Letterman, trying not to think. If he kept moving, kept talking to other people, kept the TV on, he could avoid thinking about what happened last night. And he needed not to think about that right now. Because if he thought about that, he'd want to do something really stupid and probably ruin the show. And he didn't want to ruin the show. And there was Josh too. He couldn't do this now.

Troy stared at the screen and methodically drank the beer. *Don't think, don't think,* he told himself. *Just keep doing what has to be done. Take care of Josh. Do your job. Don't let anyone down.*

He was afraid to turn off the TV because he knew what would happen if he did. He would see her face. He would hear her voice in his head. He would feel the heat in his body as it recalled how it felt to be holding her, held by her.

Because Troy had felt it. She had wanted him too. And as much as he wanted it, he was afraid to start something that was based on the make-believe world of theatre. He'd seen plenty of backstage romances vanish faster than the scenery once the show was over. People resumed their normal identities and the fairy dust of glamour that made them seem special no longer worked its magic.

Troy couldn't help thinking that if Ava admired him now it was because he was the director, the man in charge, the macho can-do guy who solves everyone's problems. But once the play was over she would see him for the ordinary guy he was. Just a blue collar guy. Not some Shakespearean guru. Just a guy with a truck. A needy lonely guy with a truck and a little boy who needed his father on date nights.

So forget it, Troy thought dully, finishing off his beer. *After next weekend it will be back to usual. Just me and David Letterman. No sense kidding myself. She was excited last night. Maybe she doesn't even remember kissing me.*

But, no matter how long he kept the TV on, Troy could think of little else.

By noon on Sunday the sun was so warm that Ava was grateful for the dappled shade behind the curtain. Popcorn clouds dotted the turquoise sky. It was a perfect day.

Ava was determined not to let anything spoil it. She blamed the other night on the mix of moonlight and champagne. Today she was clear-eyed and cool-headed. An actress with a job to do. Not a giddy girl with a crush on some pretty face. Not a Helena.

She slipped into the dressing tent, changed into her costume and carefully applied her makeup, concentrating on not thinking about anything but her lines.

When she stepped out she planned to find a quiet spot to wait for her call. She would conduct herself professionally. She found an empty chair off to one side of the stage and sat there watching the rest of the cast getting themselves together. It all seemed to be happening in slow motion, through a screen. As if someone had pressed the mute button. Then Ava noticed Troy in a cluster of people and her calm vanished. She watched him going over something with the sound engineer, while right behind him three more people were waiting to talk to him. His face wore the patient, thoughtful expression she had come to expect and her heart sank as she watched him. He wasn't some figment of moonlight and champagne. He was real, very real, and everything she admired in a man, except tall. And Ava realized that for the first time in her life, she couldn't care less. So what if he had to look up to her? She could never look down on him, not after she had come to respect and admire him so. But it was more than admiration, much more. Ava felt a dull ache in her chest and she knew it wasn't heartburn.

Later, standing in the wings, Troy watched Ava cooing lovingly to Tim in the scene where Titania is under the spell of Oberon's love potion. *That's what I need*, thought Troy. *Some trick to make her see me as a foot taller.*

Despite his feelings for her, and his hope that she was beginning to feel for him too, Troy couldn't shake the idea that Ava deserved a leading man who looked the part. In other words, someone a few inches taller. *But, it shouldn't matter, should it?* he argued with himself. *Either she likes me the way I am or she's not the woman I think she is.*

The sound of Ava's voice unlocked some space inside Troy's heart he didn't know he had. It was like when Josh was born and he found a whole new reservoir of love, different than the helpless attraction he'd always felt for Kerry. Ava was different. She made Troy feel stronger. It was something about the way she looked at him, the way she spoke his name. He could hear respect in her voice. And, lately, something more. Troy sighed as Ava caressed Bottom in his donkey's head.

When the matinee finished the sun was still high in the sky and after Ava hung up her costume she realized she had free time. *Time to run*, she thought gratefully. *That's what I need.* With all the rain in the last month Ava's marathon training had slipped and, although she was confident she could get herself ready before the November marathon, she knew running would help clear her head of other problems too.

She stopped quickly at her apartment, changed into running clothes and stretched, then headed for the park.

Seeing Ava departing from Maymont, Troy was glad he had managed to avoid saying anything stupid to her at least.

But avoiding her depressed him too. When Josh came running up to him Troy was almost relieved that he had things to do, other problems to absorb his thoughts.

"Hey Dad, you're taking me to Aunt Jenny's right? For my pickup game? Remember?"

Troy looked blank for a moment. "Oh. Yeah, right. I almost forgot." He looked at Josh for a second and smiled. "You probably ought to wipe off some of that eye makeup first, though. Or Ashley will give you a hard time."

"Who cares," said Josh, but he rubbed his sleeve across his face anyway, smearing the makeup without effectively reducing it.

After he dropped Josh off, Troy suddenly realized he was free for the rest of the afternoon, and the sun was still shining brightly. Troy drove to his apartment, changed quickly into his soccer shorts and shoes, and went to the park where he was sure the Toreadors would be playing.

"Hey Shakespeare." Carlos greeted him when he arrived. Troy grinned, although he was ready to forget about Shakespeare for a few hours at least. He trotted out on the field kicking a ball ahead of him, and for the next hour he didn't think about anything but moving to the ball.

Then, while he was staring across the field expecting a pass a blur of lime green caught his eye and he saw a tall slender woman running along the jogging trail that bordered one end of the park. Without thinking Troy started off running and in a few minutes he caught up with Ava. He fell into her rhythm, running beside her. She nodded to him briefly when he appeared, but she didn't slow her pace. She just said, "I don't like to talk when I run."

"Neither do I," he replied.

They ran side by side for two miles without speaking another word. When they came back past the soccer field again he gave her a little wave and peeled off. She waved back and kept running.

"Hey man, what happened to you? She shoot you down?" Carlos kicked a ball to Troy.

"Not my type," said Troy, trapping the ball on his chest and sending it up the field. He ran after it, and pretended to be concentrating on the game. But he wasn't fooling anyone.

For the next two days Troy threw himself into his job, working from before dawn till the sun fled the sky, trying to keep his thoughts off Ava. By the time the pickup rehearsal rolled around on Wednesday, he was worn out from trying to evade the memory of Ava in his arms.

Since the Maymont grounds weren't open late in the evening except for special events, the cast had agreed to meet at the park at dinner time to run through the play, brushing up any rough spots and tweaking the laugh lines. When Troy arrived with a sandwich and a cup of coffee at 6:00 Ava was already there, dressed in her running gear. His eyes lingered on her lean muscular legs. Troy shook himself and forced a smile.

"Hi. You already go for a run?" He felt stupid for asking such an obvious question, but being this close to her made him feel stupid.

She smiled easily. "Yeah. This weather's so great. It makes me want to run for hours." She stretched as she said this and Troy held his breath.

"Are you, I mean, do you run just for fun, or are you . . . just into fitness?" Troy stuffed his sandwich into his mouth, as if to stop the drivel coming out of it.

Ava smiled again and Troy nearly choked at the way she looked at him.

"Actually, I'm training to run in the Richmond Marathon."

"Really? Wow. Pretty intense. Have you done other marathons?"

"A couple. My dream is to one day do the Honolulu Marathon. It would be a great excuse to go to Hawaii, and it's one of the biggest and prettiest marathons." She shrugged. "It's something to do."

Troy shook his head in amazement. "I'm impressed. I've thought about doing a marathon, but it's such a commitment. I've never done more than ten miles at a stretch."

"Oh, if you can do ten you can do twenty. It's those last six that are the killers."

"I'll bet."

Most of the rest of the cast had arrived by this time, and they quickly ran through the scenes that needed attention. Troy noticed Ava getting ready to leave and he searched his mind for some plausible excuse to get her to stay, but before he could think of one she waved goodbye and drove off.

"You know, you could just ask her out," said Tim, coming up next to Troy.

"Is it that obvious?" asked Troy.

"Pretty much," said Tim.

Troy hesitated, wrinkling his forehead. "Do you think it's obvious to her?"

Tim shrugged. "Hard to say. Women always pretend like they don't notice. But I think they do."

"So maybe she's waiting for me to ask?"

"I didn't say that. I'm just saying, you two seemed to be enjoying yourselves at the cast party."

"I thought no one noticed."

"Man. Are you kidding? We talked of nothing else."

Troy looked so worried at this that Tim burst out laughing and said, "Nah. I noticed. I don't think anyone else was paying attention. And what would it matter if they did?"

"I guess it wouldn't. It's just, you know, Josh. I don't want to complicate things with his mother."

"Hey. She complicated them first right? You're entitled." Tim slapped Troy on the back. "Son, you should just call her up and ask her out. Clear the air."

"Maybe you're right. She can always say no."

Tim grinned and shook his head. "That's right. Think positive."

"Ava Morrison." Ava answered her desk phone without thinking and when she heard Troy's hurried proposal of a dinner date that night she sat back in her chair.

At first she thought she should say no. Nip this silly crush in the bud. In less than a week the play would be over and she'd never have to see him again. And that would be the sensible thing to do. It couldn't work out. They lived in two different worlds. The only one they shared was the make-believe world of theatre.

But as she sat there buying time by asking a question about the play Ava had a sudden vivid recollection of how it felt to have Troy's arms around her and his lips on hers and she heard her voice saying, "Dinner would be nice. It would be nice to get a chance to talk about something besides the play."

"Yeah. That's what I thought too," said Troy, and Ava could hear the smile in his voice.

They met at a little Italian trattoria in Carytown. They sat at a table outside under the vine-covered arbor on the brick patio. The air was soft and scented with peonies whose blowzy blooms leaned drunkenly from big tubs in the corners. Ava looked at the candlelight reflected in Troy's eyes and wondered what she was doing going out with him when she knew it couldn't work. *What girl dreams of meeting a man who is short, dark and handsome?* she thought.

After ordering a bottle of wine from the waiter, Troy turned his gaze upon her and smiled so warmly that Ava mused, *Maybe two out of three isn't so bad.*

"I've got a confession to make," said Troy. "I haven't been able to stop thinking about you since Friday night."

Ava's heart stumbled. "Oh?" she said, stalling for time.

Troy continued urgently, "I know we've only known each other a short time Ava, but I haven't felt this way about any woman since my divorce."

"Oh," said Ava, crumpling her napkin in her lap and biting her lower lip. She took a deep breath and met Troy's eyes and said, "I've been thinking about you too. I mean, Friday. It . . . was special for me too."

Troy smiled with obvious relief and Ava suddenly sensed how hard it must have been for him to work up the courage to reveal his feelings for her when they both weren't slightly loaded. He reached for her hand and Ava gave it to him and they stared at each other for a moment that stretched awkwardly between them. Finally Ava pulled her hand gently away and said, "It's been wonderful working with you in the play, but, you know, I wonder if maybe that's all it is. You know? The costumes, the lights, the excitement. If you saw me in my classroom I think you'd feel differently."

"No I wouldn't. I'd sit at the front of the class and take lots of notes and ask thoughtful, stimulating questions," said Troy.

Ava smiled. "Well, if you did that, Mr. Burnett, I would definitely have to give you a good grade."

The waiter returned with the wine and they both drank quickly from their glasses as they studied the menu.

During dinner Ava asked Troy about where he went to school, why he chose landscape design, and why he stayed in Richmond. In turn Troy questioned Ava about her world travels while growing up, how she ended up in Richmond, and why she liked to run marathons.

"There's something so pure and free about running," said Ava, as she finished her cannoli. "It's like, when I'm running I can outrun everything that has disappointed me in life."

"Has there been that much?" asked Troy gently.

Ava paused. "I guess, compared to people with real problems, no. I've been pretty lucky. But, you know, when you grow up with all these happily-ever-after expectations and then you find out that those only happen for people who can afford them, or for people who are just really lucky, then it feels, I don't know, kind of . . . I don't know. Sad, I guess."

They sat quietly for a moment.

Ava began to feel like an idiot for getting all serious when clearly Troy was trying to steer the evening in a different direction, so she shook herself and said, "I'm a lot happier since I met you." And then she stopped in surprise as she suddenly felt the truth of her words. She was happier. Sitting there with Troy glowing at her, she felt valued. And Ava recognized the buzz in her veins. It didn't come from the wine. It came from feeling desired.

Dinner was over but Troy's hunger was loud and clear in the look he gave her, and Ava felt her body responding to the call.

"Would you like to come over to my place?" asked Troy. Ava noticed that he didn't bother to make up some plausible excuse for why she should come and she was glad that he didn't insult her by pretending he wanted simply to continue their discussion. She knew what he wanted. And she wanted it too.

But, a few moments later as they climbed the stairs to Troy's apartment, Ava began to wonder if maybe things weren't moving a little too fast.

Then Troy opened the door and she walked in and her anxiety vanished at the unexpected sight of a large indoor jungle dominating Troy's living room.

"What is that?" she asked.

"Oh. That's Hobbes' cage. I guess I didn't tell you about Hobbes. He's Josh's iguana. He was really little when we bought him, but he's gotten too big for a glass case anymore, so I built this for him last winter. He seems to like it. And it's easier to clean."

Ava peered in past the palm fronds and large rocks. "Is he in there now?"

Troy came over close to her and looked in. "Yeah. There he is. He stretches out on that branch under the heat lamp most of the time. He doesn't move around much."

Looking closer Ava saw a lizard almost the size of a small cat sleeping on the driftwood perch. "He looks like he's smiling in his sleep."

"Yeah. Hobbes is pretty easy going. He gets nervous when Simon scratches his paws on the cage, but I made sure Simon can't get in."

"And Simon is?"

"My cat."

Ava nodded. "Josh told me he wants a dog."

Troy shook his head. "Yeah. I know. I'd like to get him one, but this apartment's just too small, and I'm not here enough. Dogs get lonely. Not like cats."

Ava wondered if it had been a mistake to come to Troy's place. Seeing him here with his son's pet and the Nintendo games on the coffee table and the kind of free flowing mess that she never allowed in her own carefully arranged apartment, she suddenly felt out of place. But before she had time to say anything Troy grabbed her hand and pulled her toward the couch. "Come here," he said, pushing onto the floor the magazines and newspapers that covered the couch.

She let herself be led and when he sat down and pulled her toward him she didn't resist. He looked at her with heat in his eyes and she leaned into his kiss. She stopped thinking and let herself enjoy the feeling of his hands moving on her body. It had been such a long time since she had let herself go with anyone. And Troy wasn't just anyone. When his lips left hers he started kissing her neck and she felt her body responding with an eagerness she could hardly contain.

"Oh," she gasped, lifting her hips against him. He pressed against her, his hands inflaming her. He started to pull at the buttons on her blouse and she was fumbling for his when the shrill ring of the phone startled them and they fell off the couch together, landing on the rug laughing.

"I'm not answering that," he muttered softly, pulling her closer.

"Good," she said.

Then, as the answering machine clicked on a woman's voice burst angrily into the quiet room. "Troy, are you there? You'd better pick up the phone if you are. I've just been hearing from Josh about how you've dragged him into this play of yours and you better believe I am not happy about it."

Troy looked at Ava's startled eyes for a second, then he climbed quickly over the couch and picked up the phone. "Kerry? Kerry, calm down. There's no reason to get excited."

From the floor where she sat feeling dazed Ava could hear the woman on the other end of the line shrieking. Every few minutes Troy would begin, "Kerry, if you'd just listen to me . . ." And then the woman would rant for another minute. As her pulse slowed, Ava buttoned her blouse and got up.

"It's Shakespeare, Kerry. It's not perverted." He rolled his eyes at Ava as he said this. She smiled wanly. "I know, I know." He shook his head. "You know, I really don't care what Gary said." Now he was frowning, clenching his fist. Ava felt sorry for him, but she suddenly felt that the phone call was a sign for her to leave. What had she been thinking? They still had two performances of the play to do. It would be crazy to start sleeping with the director now.

She caught Troy's eye and mouthed, "Goodbye."

He mouthed, "Don't go."

But she just stretched her lips in a tight smile and backed away. When she got outside the door she could still hear Troy inside pleading, "Listen Kerry. That's not what it is."

Ava hurried out onto the street and walked quickly back to her car parked near the restaurant. She breathed deeply, feeling an odd combination of relief and disappointment. She got in her car and sighed. She turned the key in the ignition and turned on the radio and the oldies hour on Q101 blared out Linda Rondstadt singing, "When will I be loved?" Ava snorted cynically as she stepped on the gas. *Not tonight sweetheart*, she thought.

Chapter Eleven

When Ava got to her office the next morning on her desk was a large vase of deep lavender roses, their musky fragrance filling the small room. The card tucked into the flowers read, "For Titania, who rules my heart. Troy."

She smiled and sat down, wondering if maybe she shouldn't have run off so quickly last night. Then she remembered the harried look on Troy's face as he tried to reason with his ex-wife. *Poor thing, no wonder he's stayed single*, she thought.

"Wow, somebody likes you," said Chenille, poking her head in the door.

Ava grinned.

"How'd the date go?"

Ava shrugged. "It was going almost too well until his ex-wife called right when we were getting to the best part."

"Oh? And where were you when this happened?"

"At his place."

"Ooh, Ave. I'm so happy for you. He seems like such a nice guy."

"Yeah. He does. I keep wondering when the mask is going to slip. Nobody can be as nice as he is."

"Well, he is kind of short. Maybe he has to be nice."

"Because?"

"Because he can't intimidate anyone, not being a gorilla like some guys we know."

"Hmm. Maybe." Ava leaned into the flowers and breathed deeply. "Maybe he's just one of the really rare ones. A nice guy who is single because he's too nice to ask anyone to deal with his kid and his shrewish ex-wife."

Chenille considered this. "Well, I hope you're right."

"How about you? Have you figured out your strategy for Howie?"

Chenille walked over to the window. "You know, I need him to see me first."

"See you?"

"Yes. Like across a crowded room kind of thing."

"Oh really? I guess you should have come to the cast party."

"Yes, well, I was hoping you'd ask."

"Oh, Nille, I'm so sorry. I've been so selfish. I wasn't thinking."

Chenille nodded, her blonde curls softly bobbing. "It's okay, Ave. He probably would have been too full of himself that night anyway. I need to get him when he's not so cocky."

Ava snorted. "Well good luck." Then she remembered seeing Howard getting shot down by the little redheaded fairy. "Actually, you might be right. I don't know. I think there's supposed to be another cast party after the final performance on Saturday."

"And you won't forget me this time," smiled Chenille.

"Not a chance," said Ava.

"All righty then. Some enchanted evening here I come."

Ava grinned. Whether it was the roses or Chenille's serene romantic faith or the still warm memory of last night, Ava felt more optimistic about life in general than she had in years, and her students that afternoon sat up in wonder as she lectured with uncharacteristic verve and humor on the foibles of the post modernists.

Walking home later, with the sunlight spilling through the

trees that canopied Monument Avenue, Ava felt like skipping. She hurried up the stairs to her apartment, ate a quick
yogurt, made herself a tall latte to go, and drove across town
to Maymont.

The place was buzzing. The good weather, good reviews,
and strong word-of-mouth on campus had brought the
biggest crowd yet. The Maymont officials were beside themselves, enthusiastically talking about making the play an annual fundraiser for the park.

Ava looked around for Troy when she got backstage but
couldn't see him anywhere. She did notice Josh, standing at
the front of the stage area talking with a very attractive
woman. Standing next to the woman was a man wearing a
garish jacket completely covered with corporate logos. Ava
suddenly realized the woman must be Josh's mother, and
judging by the way Josh was staring at the grass and looking
uncomfortable Ava guessed his mother wasn't giving him
any encouragement.

Ava wanted to go over and say something but she didn't
have any idea what. Before she could think of anything to do
Alex appeared next to Josh and must have said something to
give Josh an excuse to get away. The woman and her escort
laughed together after Alex and Josh left, and Ava had a bad
feeling as she watched them settle down on a blanket near
the front of the stage.

That night the show began slowly, as usual. No one worried about the rocky first scene because they all had confidence in the rest of the play. But when Heather slipped on
the dewy grass and fell when she made her first entrance,
and the audience roared when the actors weren't trying to
get laughs, a fissure of doubt opened, and that was only the
beginning.

The first chilling realization that Heather's slip had been
only the first pebble in an avalanche of missed cues and
mishaps came when the mechanicals began their vaude-
villian routine, which usually went as smoothly as soft shoe.

But tonight it was all stubbed toes and dropped lines. When Tim finally came off stage he shook his head and said grimly to Ava, "Well, we were due. Got to expect at least one off night. We'll just have to ride it out."

The anticipation of trouble seemed a self-fulfilling prophecy from that point on. Thankfully, the audience didn't seem to know, or care. They cheered and hooted at every laugh line, and at many lines that were supposed to be appreciated for other merits.

Ava caught sight of Troy watching during her first scene and the troubled expression on his face made her forget her next line. She struggled to get back on course, hoping that the worst was over.

From the audience she kept hearing some man guffawing loudly every time Oberon said a word, and she had a sickening feeling that if she looked out there it would be the logo guy, who had the look of a natural born heckler. She tried to concentrate, to stay in character. When they got to the scene where Bottom is wearing the donkey's head and Titania is fawning all over him, Ava clasped the furry head to kiss it, as she had done during every other performance. But, in every other performance, the donkey head had remained on Tim's shoulders. Tonight, it came off in Ava's hands.

The audience howled. Tim looked at her wild-eyed. Ava held the big donkey head and blurted, "Oh. I'm so sorry."

Tim put his hands to his head and ad-libbed, "It's Excedrin headache number twenty-nine."

The audience roared.

Tim wailed, "I've lost my head."

"Here," said Ava, trying to put the donkey's head back on Tim.

Tim resisted. "That's not my head."

Ava looked perplexed for a second, then she said, "Oh, but my dear sweet lord, it looks so well on you. Please do put it on for me."

Tim appeared to be thinking this over. He gave the audience a waggish look and wiggled his eyebrows. "Methinks if doth please the lady, I would do well to wear the hairy head. Mayhaps I'll get lucky."

So saying this he took the head and put it back on and the scene finished more or less as Shakespeare wrote it, but when Ava came off to the wings she was sweating and trembling.

"Oh god! That was horrible," she gasped.

Nina patted her on the back and said, "It could have been worse. You handled it all right."

Ava shook her head. Tim was already laughing about it with the other actors backstage, but for Ava the panicky moment onstage had left her feeling breathless and shaken. She looked for Troy, but when she saw him on the other side of the stage she realized immediately that he was dealing with problems of his own.

Josh was sitting on the grass shaking his head. Alex and Troy appeared to be trying to persuade him to do something.

"What's going on over there?" whispered Ava to Nina.

Nina glanced across the stage. "Josh's mother just told him that only a sissy would pretend to be a fairy and that if he does all his friends will think he's a wimp."

Ava looked shocked. "You're kidding!"

"I wish. Sadly, there are a lot of people who think that way."

"Man. What kind of a mother would do that?"

Nina shrugged. "She probably thinks she's doing the right thing. I just feel sorry for Troy, having to put up with that woman."

"I don't understand how he ever married her."

Nina looked skeptically at Ava. "Have you seen her? He was just a kid when they met. She was a cheerleader. He's only human."

Ava frowned. *Right. He's only human. So?* she thought. *Why is it everyone makes excuses for men when they act like idiots?* Across the stage she watched as Troy hugged his red-faced son and she felt a wave of compassion for them both.

When the show finally ended Ava took her bows and looked around to see if Troy was waiting for her anywhere, but he and Josh had vanished. Ava drove slowly home alone with the windows open in her car, listening to the sirens in the distance. She thought about Josh trying to make sense of the crazy mixed signals from his mother and father, not to mention his mother's boyfriend. No wonder the kid preferred soccer. The rules were clear on the field. Plus, there was a referee to keep things from getting too far out of hand.

Ava fumed thinking about how Josh's mother had tried to make the boy feel ashamed of wearing tights. Ava thought about the little boy who'd told her of his longing for a puppy, and she wished she could help Troy comfort him now. *After all*, she thought, *lots of famous, important men wore tights. Like Louis the XIV, and Shakespeare, and . . . Robin Hood!* Ava wished she could call Josh right now and remind him of Robin Hood. *Nobody was cooler than Robin Hood. Hah.*

The next morning Ava called Chenille and asked if she wanted a ride to the play. "I figure you're hoping you'll be riding with Howard by the end of the night, right? So you won't want to be worrying about your car."

"Thanks Ave, but actually, I've already got it covered. I've got a whole bunch of my students coming tonight. I told them there would be extra credit questions on the exams next week and anyone who wanted to do well would be smart to come to the play."

"Oh, clever. I wish I'd thought of that."

"Yeah. So, a couple of the girls are giving me a ride."

"Great. And I'll give you a lift to the cast party."

"I'm counting on it."

As Ava slipped into her Titania gown for the final performance she felt a rush of wistfulness. It would all be over in just a few hours. She wished she could slow time and make this night last longer. But of course, by the law of inverse desires, the minutes raced by and before she had another moment to reflect she was waiting in the wings for her entrance cue.

The lawn was packed and the audience was responsive. A cool breeze sprang up in the second act and continued, getting stronger as the evening went on. By intermission a damp heaviness in the air hinted at rain. A low rumble of distant thunder heightened the drama of Oberon's entrance in the fourth act and the audience murmured appreciatively.

The breeze began gusting stronger in the last act. Errant paper cups and programs skipped along the grass. The temperature fell dramatically and several people in the audience gathered their belongings and began heading for the parking lot, glancing apprehensively at the threatening sky as they went.

A sense of foreboding gathered in the air and a note of urgency crept into Nigel's voice as he tried to finish the final poetic lines, but before he could, a crack of lightning ripped open the sky and rain thrashed down on the stage drowning all other sound.

The lights went out immediately and in the dark and wet chaos the stage crew scrambled to try to cover their equipment while the actors ran for cover. Ava saw Josh looking scared and alone by the dressing tent. She grabbed his hand and shouted above the storm, "Come on. We'll be safe in your dad's truck."

"I'm supposed to stay here. I'm supposed to meet my dad by the tent," wailed Josh.

"He wouldn't want you to be out in this," yelled Ava. Josh looked around frantically as another explosion of lightning lit up the grounds. Then, reluctantly, not seeing Troy anywhere, he ran through the slashing rain with Ava to the truck which was parked in the lot closest to the dressing tent. By the time they reached the truck they were both soaked. They climbed inside and slammed the door behind them. The rain pounding on the truck roof sounded like a kettle drum. Ava smiled at Josh. "We'll be okay in here. It's the safest place to be in a thunderstorm."

Josh didn't look entirely convinced, but he edged closer to Ava and looked at the rain sheeting over the windshield. "I hope my dad is okay."

"He'll be fine. I'm sure he knows what to do," said Ava, hoping she wasn't wrong.

They sat and listened to the storm for a minute. Josh fidgeted slightly against Ava.

"My dad said I was supposed to wait by the tent."

Ava rubbed her hands against her wet arms. The rain was cold and the heat of the day was long gone.

"I'm sure he wouldn't have wanted you to wait for him there in this storm," she said. She reached out and pushed Josh's wet hair off his face. He looked up at her gravely. "He'll probably be here as soon as the storm lets up," she said.

An icy shard of lightning lit the truck cab and Josh flinched. The drilling rain showed no signs of abating soon, and as the minutes went by Ava tried not to let her growing unease show. Troy would be there soon. She was sure of it.

Then, with the suddenness of a lightning strike the truck door behind Josh yanked open filling the cab with the sound of roaring rain, but louder than that was Troy's voice. "Where have you been!" he yelled. "I told you to wait by the tent! I've been looking everywhere! You scared me to death. Why didn't you do what I told you?"

Josh cowered closer to Ava and mumbled. "Ava said I'd be safe here."

Only then did Troy look up and see Ava staring at him in alarm.

"Who told you to take my son?" shouted Troy, glaring at her. "Who do you think you are? I've got enough to worry about! I don't need you to take care of my son."

Ava lowered her head and tried to talk softly, reasonably, but the rain made it impossible. "I'm sorry. I thought I was helping," she shouted.

"I don't need your help," yelled Troy, shaking with anger. "You haven't got a clue about what it means to be a parent.

You're so self-absorbed you couldn't take care of a goldfish. Just leave my son alone from now on!"

Ava's face flamed with heat and she could feel tears rising. She pushed hard on the door behind her and ran out into the storm. She ran all the way to her car, which was parked in the lot farthest from the stage area. She leaped inside it and sat staring numbly at the veil of rain on the windshield. When her heart had slowed slightly she lifted her chin and found her keys which she had hidden under the seat. She started the car and drove home trying not to think at all. She channeled the quiet storm of rage building inside her, focusing on driving carefully through the lashing rain. She managed to contain the tears until she finally collapsed inside the door of her apartment, wet cold and more miserable than she had ever been in her life.

The next morning a soft sunlight streamed across the bare pale oak floors of Ava's apartment. When she opened her eyes she felt curiously drained and blank. Then the memory of Troy's words jabbed through the fog of sleep and Ava was wide awake, hurt, and angry. As she made herself a cup of espresso she went over the whole scene in her mind and couldn't find a single reason to forgive Troy. She winced as she remembered how his face had looked, contorted with rage. She shivered slightly in the warm sunlight. The deep quiet of her apartment, the soothing sight of her carefully arranged art works and her minimalist furnishings surrounded Ava with a sense of the identity she'd almost left behind during these crowded months of play rehearsals.

She breathed deeply and went through her pre-run stretching routine almost without thinking. Only once did a merry bubble of memory slip into her consciousness, as she thought of Iris skipping across the stage. Ava shook her head to restore her clarity. *It was all just A Midsummer Night's Dream after all,* she decided. *And now I've woken up, and the guy I thought was a prince among men turns out to be an ass just like all the rest.*

Hmmph, she sniffed. *Now I really know how Titania felt.*

Ava laced up her running shoes and headed outside. She had a marathon to run, and if she just kept running, she hoped, she could outrun those foolish lying memories.

She set off down Monument but when she came to the turn to get to the park and her usual route, she veered in the opposite direction. She wasn't going to take any chance of running into Troy on the soccer field again. Even if he wanted to apologize, Ava wasn't sure she wanted to hear it. *Maybe it's better this way,* she thought grimly. *It's not like we were made for each other.*

As Ava sprinted out of range the phone in her apartment rang. Troy hung up when he heard the answering machine click on. He didn't want to apologize on tape. He needed to hear her voice.

Ever since Ava had disappeared into the rain last night Troy had been kicking himself for losing his temper. He'd been so frantic to find Josh that when he got to the truck his relief at finding him turned instantly into anger, the way his mother used to yell at him when he came home late after making her worry. He knew she didn't mean it, that it was just a measure of how worried she'd been. But, Troy knew he had no right to vent his distress on Ava. And he'd done worse than that. He'd insulted her cruelly. It would serve him right if she never spoke to him again. Troy couldn't accept that fate without at least trying to earn her forgiveness.

He called three times that morning before Josh insisted that they had to go to the park.

"Maybe Ava will be there, Dad," said Josh.

Troy hoped so.

But, though they hung around the park for more than four hours, playing soccer and practicing, they never saw Ava. She carefully skirted the park as she ran her five miles, and by the time she returned to her apartment she felt tired and cleansed. When she saw the red message light blinking as she came in Ava was tempted to erase it without listening, fearing it might be Troy and that the sound of his voice would undo all her hard work.

Come on Ava, don't be such a wimp. You've got an erase button and you know how to use it, she thought.

She poured herself half a glass of cold coffee, dumped in a large spoonful of sugar and filled the rest with milk. Stirring it, she pushed the replay.

"Ava where are you? Where were you? You didn't come to the cast party. I looked for you, but then, well, I have so much to tell you. Call me. It was great. I hope you're happy too. Bye."

Chenille's breathless message was the only one on the tape and Ava sat down and absorbed this fact as she sipped her cold latte. A nagging little disappointment pinched her throat, but she gritted her teeth and shook it off as she dialed Chenille's number.

"Ava! Where have you been? I've been dying to tell you about last night!"

Ava smiled despite her own misery. Chenille sounded like she'd been inhaling helium. "So? I'm listening."

"Oh Ave. It was so incredible! You know, right when the lightning struck, I ran backstage to find you, but then the lights went out and the rain was so loud and everyone was yelling and I was standing there wondering whether I shouldn't just run for the parking lot when all of sudden he was there. Howard. And he wrapped his cloak around me and said in that deep voice, 'Come with me. I'll take care of you.' And I looked up and there he was, with those eyes, you know, and that chin and those shoulders!"

"Yeah, I've seen them. So Howard rescued you?"

"That was how it started."

"There's more?"

"Oh my god. So much more!"

Ava laughed. She snuggled down in the couch and kicked off her shoes. "Tell me all."

Chenille giggled. "Well, really Ava, I know it happened kind of fast, but you know, it just seemed like it was destiny.

I mean, there he was and there I was, and there was this electricity between us."

"You don't think it was the lightning?"

"Oh Ave, I'm not kidding! It was like, everything slowed down around us and we were in this little capsule of, like, intensity. He was looking in my eyes like nobody has ever looked in my eyes, and I was like melting in his arms. Oh my god. It was so great."

"And all this happened while you were standing in the pouring rain?"

"No. Of course not. First he helped me to his car and we sat there for a while until the storm passed. And we talked. And everything he said just moved me. And he was asking me about my feelings and he was so gentle and respectful."

"Respectful? Are you sure it was Howard?"

"Honestly Ava, it was like some kind of . . ."

"Some enchanted evening?"

"Yes! Honest to god. And I know he felt the same way. We were both kind of, you know, like Meg Ryan and Tom Hanks in *Sleepless in Seattle* when he finally sees her up on the roof of the Empire State building and they know that they're meant for each other and they don't even say anything because they're both kind of amazed that it's happened?"

"Yeah. I love that scene."

"Me too. Well it was like that, only without the kid. Which made things easier. Because once the storm let up we went to the cast party and we had some drinks and we laughed a lot. Honestly, I don't know when I've laughed so much. And he seemed so happy to be with me. And, well, it pretty much went on like that all night." She paused and Ava took a sip from her coffee.

"All night?" she finally asked.

"Yep. Pretty much. He came to my place." She paused.

"And you . . . ?"

"And he stayed and I made him breakfast this morning and he just left around noon."

"Wow." Ava looked around her spare apartment as she put

her empty glass down, and felt a stab of envy at Chenille's fullness. Then she felt guilty for being so selfish. "That's amazing Nille. I'm so happy for you."

"Thanks. I really feel like this might be it, you know? I mean, nothing has ever felt so right."

Ava had to smile. "Well nobody deserves it more." She cradled one of the decorative pillows on the couch to her chest and asked, "So is he supposed to call you?"

"No. We already made plans to go to lunch on Wednesday."

"Really! Well, it must be love then."

There was a moment of silence during which Ava imagined Chenille's face shining with romantic bliss.

"Oh Ave! I'm sorry. I haven't even asked how your night went. Where did you go? Did you and Troy . . . ?"

Ava pressed the pillow tighter to her aching chest and said, "It's over, Nille. It wasn't meant to be." And as briefly as she could, Ava sketched out the sudden burst of temper that had doused the flickering romance.

"Oh I'm so sorry, Ava. I'll bet he's sorry too. I'm sure he'll apologize. He's probably been trying to call you all day like I have."

"I don't think so, Nille. It's okay. I'm used to being alone. Maybe . . . I don't know." Ava paused, remembering Troy's stinging remark about her inability to care for so much as a pet. She had left that part out when she told Chenille about the scene.

"Don't give up, Ava. If Troy isn't smart enough to appreciate you, then he wasn't the one after all. So don't worry."

"I'm not worried," Ava replied. She hung up the phone and sat in the still quiet of her apartment. Outside on the street she could see the late afternoon light gilding the trees on Monument. She stared out the window for a while, then put her head in her hands, shut her eyes, and wept.

Chapter Twelve

The next morning Ava got up early, took her five-mile jog around the park, came back, got dressed, stopped for coffee, and went to her office. While she was running off study guides on the copier, Deirdre Finch bustled past the doorway with a large cardboard box. A moment later she reappeared. "Ava? I didn't expect to see you here today. Your classes are over, aren't they?"

"Yes. I'm just taking care of some late papers." Ava noticed that the large box Deirdre was carrying seemed to be moving. "What's in the box?"

"Puppies. Want one?" Deirdre edged closer so Ava could see into the box, where six tiny brown and white furballs were climbing over one another.

"They look like hamsters," said Ava.

Deirdre laughed. "Yes, well, they should have been Jack Russell terriers, which is what their mother is, but we think the father was a beagle that belongs to one of our neighbors. So they're going to run all day and bark all night."

Ava watched the puppies wiggling and wriggling, biting and climbing over each other. Their nonstop motion was oddly hypnotic.

Deirdre said, "I was just kidding, of course. You're not a pet person, are you?"

Ava flinched. She reached into the box to touch one of the puppies and it licked her hand. She lifted it out of the box and held it closer to her face, examining its bright brown eyes and funny little grin. It wagged its tail furiously and tried to reach her face with its tongue. Ava laughed.

She looked at Deirdre who was watching her carefully. "They are cute," said Ava. She brought the puppy closer to her face and it licked her cheek. She was surprised to find that instead of being repulsed by this, she liked it. "Hey, not on the first date," she said to the puppy.

Deirdre set the box down on edge of the copier. "He's going to need an owner who can give him lots of exercise," she said. "Jack Russells can run all day. Seriously."

"Really?" said Ava, studying the tiny mutt. "His legs are so short."

"Yes. Jack Russells all have short legs, but they have incredible energy. They really belong in the country, or somewhere they can get a lot of room to run."

Ava started to put the puppy back in the box, but as she did so it scrambled for purchase on her arm, trying to claw its way up.

"Looks like he doesn't want to let you go," laughed Deirdre.

Ava paused. Deirdre's turn of phrase had struck a nerve and it was all Ava could do to keep from bursting into tears in front of her. She swallowed hard and grasped the puppy in her hand. It squirmed happily in her palm.

"I was just kidding, Ava," said Deirdre, reaching for the puppy. "I don't want to pressure you into taking a pet you don't want. Dogs can be a lot of work if you're not used to it. Like kids."

Ava winced and held the puppy closer while it nibbled on her thumb. She looked at Deirdre and said, "What should I feed it?"

Deirdre grinned. She gave Ava a detailed list of supplies she would need, and the name of a vet for the puppy's shots, and a few minutes later Ava was driving home with the puppy scrabbling and whining noisily inside the cardboard box Ava had put him in to keep him from getting under her feet while she drove.

Ava's second thoughts didn't chime in until she had the puppy in her apartment and confronted the messy business of newspapers and housetraining. But the process kept her so absorbed that it wasn't until she had Zoom settled in his sleeping box that she thought to look at her answering machine. It was blinking furiously. Ava took a deep breath and sat down next to it before she summoned the will to punch the replay.

"Ava? Ava, it's me. Please call me. I need to talk to you." Troy's voice brought the tears up to her throat, but she clenched her fists and fought her own weakness. *Don't wait up,* she thought bitterly.

"Ava, please. Call me."

She angrily punched the button.

The next message began with a five second pause, then Troy's quiet voice said softly, "Please forgive me, Ava. I never meant to say those things to you. I was out of my mind with worry but I know that's no excuse. I don't blame you for being mad. But please give me another chance. Call me."

Ava sat very still, breathing shallowly. She looked at the time on the answering machine. He'd called at noon. She got up and paced around the room. The phone tempted her like a box of chocolates. *Right, all I have to do is call you and we can get back to whatever it was we were trying to do. Which was what?*

"And why do you care, Ava?" she said aloud to herself. She sat down and held her head in her hands wretchedly. *I wish I didn't care,* she thought miserably.

She lifted her head at a skittering sound on the floor and saw that Zoom had woken from his mini-nap and was trying to get her to play, biting her shoes and jumping on them. She smiled and picked him up.

"Okay baby, it's just you and me. Wanna go for a run?"

Zoom wriggled happily in her hands and Ava turned her back on the phone and put her running shoes back on and went to the park, confident that Troy wouldn't be there in the middle of a work day.

Zoom loved the park. He ran in dizzying circles around Ava as she jogged and he never fell behind, though he took numerous detours to sniff at the marks left by other dogs, and to chase the waddling pigeons. Ava ran for two hours and by the time she and Zoom returned to her apartment she had made up her mind not to call Troy. The play was over. The school semester was over. She would need all summer to train for the marathon and if she ran out of things to do, well, maybe she would go for a vacation. Go to the beach, or visit her parents. She could take Zoom. She would never be lonely again.

When Ava didn't return his calls, Troy felt baffled. He knew he'd hurt her. He hoped she'd forgive him after she'd had time. But as the days passed and still she didn't call, he began to worry that she had decided to forget him. And he could not forget her.

Each day he woke with his hope slightly renewed. By nature an optimist, he took strength from the sunlight, the beauty of growing things, the faith and love of his son. Josh kept urging his father to call Ava.

"I've called her, Josh. She won't call me back."

"Well you should go see her, Dad." Josh sat on the couch in Troy's apartment stroking Simon who was staring lazily into the iguana cage. "Maybe you could take her a goldfish."

Troy's eyebrows flexed with confusion.

"You know. You told her she couldn't take care of a goldfish. So you could give her one to show that you didn't mean it."

Troy hung his head. He'd forgotten, or maybe suppressed would be a better word, the memory of what he'd said to Ava that night. *I'll bet she hasn't forgotten a single word*, he thought.

"I don't know Josh. She might not want to have to take care of a fish tank."

"How about a puppy? Everybody likes puppies," said Josh, smiling winningly.

Troy laughed. "Everyone but your mom."

"Right."

Troy finished wrapping the peanut butter sandwiches he was preparing to take to the park. "I know how much you liked Ava. And I really like her too. But sometimes things just don't work out between people. And maybe Ava doesn't want to be friends with me anymore."

Josh looked skeptically at Troy. "I don't want her to be just a friend."

Troy sighed. "I don't either," he said.

When the weekend arrived Troy felt hopeful that somehow enough time had passed that Ava would be receptive to his apology. Also, Troy thought the chances of running into Ava at the park would be better on a Saturday.

But, his optimism faded after a morning spent scanning the jogging path. Troy tried to keep up a show of carefree athletic activity, but around noon Josh headed for the side of the field and stopped running.

"What's up Josh? You get a cramp?"

Josh frowned. "Dad, this just isn't working. I think Ava's not coming cause she knows we'll be here."

Troy looked back at the field where a half dozen of the Toreadors were dodging and weaving past one another. He sighed. "Well. Maybe you're right. But I don't see what we can do about it, do you?"

Josh balanced one foot on top of his soccer ball, and rolled it back and forth for a minute. Then he said, "I don't see why we can't go over to her apartment and tell her we're sorry and that we miss her."

Troy tried to think of some reason he could give Josh that would make sense to a seven-year-old.

"*We*, huh?"

"Yeah. You miss her. I miss her. Are we never going to see her again now that the play's over?"

Troy kneeled down and put his hands on Josh's thin upper arms. He looked him squarely in the eye. "No. We're going to see her again. I promise."

Josh set his small chin at an upward tilt and nodded his head. "Okay. But don't wait too long, okay, Dad? She could find some other boyfriend."

Troy smiled. "Not if I find her first," he said.

"Ooooh, who's this?" squealed Chenille, stepping gingerly into Ava's apartment while Zoom buzzed around her ankles.

"That's Zoom, the new love of my life," called Ava from the kitchen.

"Oh he's adorable! What is he?"

Ava explained Zoom's high-test lineage while she finished bringing dinner to the table.

"So, let me get this straight. You've never had a pet in your whole life and now suddenly you've got this high maintenance little roadrunner?" asked Chenille.

Ava poured two glasses of wine before she spoke. Then, lifting her glass she said, "I've decided that, on the whole, I prefer the company of Zoom to any man I know. He may bark a lot, but at least he never snaps at me."

Chenille drank from her glass and smiled warmly at Ava, but she shook her head.

"Oh Ava. I just think you're making a big mistake to give up on Troy."

Ava sniffed. "I didn't give up on him. He told me to butt out of his life. And that's what I'm doing."

"Hasn't he called?"

"He's tried."

"What do you mean?"

"I mean, he's left messages. None of which, I might add, were particularly compelling." Ava took a big gulp of Merlot. "The thing is, Nille. If he is supposed to be the man in my life, I mean, *The Man*, in my life, then he's got to show me something besides, 'oh, I'm sorry I yelled at you for nothing.'"

Ava shook her head again and grew more serious. "I mean it Nille. I was really, well, I was really thinking it might be . . . something special. And then I saw this side of him that I didn't know could even be there, you know? And now, I just don't know if I want to trust myself with him again. I mean, I'd rather be alone than have someone taking out his problems on me. I mean, I've got problems too, but do I take them out on other people?"

Chenille frowned. "I see. So, because he's not perfect, you're letting him go. The first guy you've cared about in, what is it, six years?"

Ava scowled. "Just because I'm picky doesn't mean I have to settle for the first guy who buys me flowers."

Chenille shrugged. "They were really nice flowers."

Chenille looked across the room where Zoom was busy tearing up a magazine that had fallen on the floor. Ava didn't seem to notice. Her usually immaculate apartment definitely had a more lived-in look thanks to the puppy, Chenille noted. She took a deep breath and said, "Listen Ava, I understand how hurt you must have been. But, you know, you have to forgive people for things. It's like Don Henley says."

Ava frowned. "I'm sorry?"

"Don Henley? The Eagles? You know that song about forgiveness? 'You keep carrying that anger, it'll eat you up inside?'"

Ava did a slight eyeroll.

"Oh come on, Ava. I know you don't believe in pop music

psychology, but it's true. I think Troy really cares for you. And you like him too. And if you let this chance go by, who knows if you'll meet another one?"

Ava frowned and stood up. "Honestly Chenille. If I wanted this kind of advice I could have invited my mother. Although, admittedly, she probably wouldn't quote Don Henley at me."

The room got very quiet and Ava felt instantly remorseful.

"I'm sorry. I'm sorry, Nille. I'm a terrible person and you're a good friend to try to cheer me up."

Chenille raised her head and lifted her wineglass. "Okay. Let's start over. To whatever Ava wants."

Ava smiled. "To whatever Ava wants."

They drank and Ava served spinach lasagna while Chenille regaled her with the latest developments in the romance with Howard.

"So it's still going great huh?"

"Oh yeah. Honestly Ava, he's hinted at marriage. And I don't think it would be too far a stretch."

Ava's eyes widened. "Marriage! You've only known him, what? Two weeks?"

Chenille's eyes took on that gooey light that Ava recognized from countless discussions with her on the subjects of love at first sight, destiny, and mad romance. "The length of time is irrelevant," asserted Chenille. "You know that. It only takes a heartbeat to fall in love."

Ava laughed softly. "Well, I guess if you look at it that way maybe you guys are meant for each other.

Chenille smiled dreamily. "I think we are."

Ava felt a pang of envy, but she smothered it in chocolate mousse with whipped cream, the next best thing to mad romance in her book.

Later, after Chenille had gone home, Ava curled up on the couch with Zoom in her lap. She looked at the phone and realized there had been no new messages from Troy for the past several days. She wondered if he'd given up. *He couldn't have cared very much if he gave up so easily,* she thought. *He knows where I live.*

Zoom wriggled in her lap, stood up, shook himself, turned around, and resettled cozily against Ava's cotton sweater.

"That's it little guy. Rest up. We've got a big day tomorrow," she murmured. She idly watched the phone as if willing it to ring. Several silent moments passed. Then without consciously examining her motives, Ava got up and began opening drawers and looking through the papers on her desk, seeking the cast list with phone numbers that had been handed out months ago when rehearsals first began. She scanned the list rapidly, then took a deep breath and picked up the phone. She quickly dialed Troy's number. If she hesitated for an instant all would be lost, she knew.

"Hello?" The woman's warm voice on the line was so unexpected that Ava nearly hung up without a word, but a desperate hope that maybe she had misdialed led her to ask, "Is Troy there?"

"No, I'm sorry. He's out. Would you like to leave a message?"

Ava shut her eyes, imagining the pretty face that must accompany such a sweet voice. "No. No, that's okay. I'll call another time." She dropped the receiver and stood in the dark, cursing herself. *You fool. He wanted to apologize, but you didn't give him a chance. And now he's found someone else.*

Or someone else found him, more likely, she thought bitterly, thinking how lonely Troy seemed and how easily a woman could take advantage of that.

Ava returned to the couch and Zoom wriggled next to her, nipping at her hands and trying to play. "Okay. I guess it's puppy love for me," said Ava, cuddling him closer. And when Zoom licked a tear off Ava's cheek, she smiled sadly and said, "Thanks. I needed that."

Returning from the video store Troy walked in and his sister and Josh met him at the door.

"Did you get it, Dad?" asked Josh bouncing on his toes.

"Yeah, they only had one copy but I got it," said Troy, sliding a DVD of *Bend it Like Beckham* on the counter.

Josh grabbed the disc and hurried to the DVD player.

"Thanks for staying with him while I went, Jen. The lines are so long on Saturdays it's easier if I go alone," said Troy.

"No problem," said Jen, sliding into her windbreaker. "Oh, some woman called for you. But she didn't leave a message. Said she'd call back."

Troy frowned. "She didn't leave a name?"

"No. She just said she'd call another time."

Troy hadn't quite given up expecting Ava to call. But, if she heard his sister's voice she might jump to the wrong conclusion. He dialed her number quickly, but when the answering machine kicked in he hung up without a word.

Chapter Thirteen

The last week of May passed in a blur of motion for Ava. With no classes to teach and the play behind her, she was free to concentrate on training for the marathon. The weather in June settled into an idyllic routine of azure skies and moderate temperatures, no humidity to speak of. Each day Ava got up, stretched, took Zoom for a brisk five-mile run around the park, then ate some lunch and stretched some more. She spent an hour in the afternoon working out in the gym. Each night she ate pasta, salad, and fruit. She drank water constantly. She did not think about Troy.

Much.

Even when she was running his face would flash before her mind's eye and she had a hard time tuning out the memory of his arms around her and his lips, the soft warmth of his lips. But in a way the memories drove her to train harder. She ran longer, faster, as if to escape them. At least the daily physical workout left her so exhausted that by nightfall she was able to sleep without too many weepy moments. She made herself a new running tape and pounded along the cinder paths by the river to the beat of Destiny's Child.

Ava let her mind empty. She welcomed the wordless space she entered when her heart rate rose and her breath pumped a steady backbeat to the meter of her shoes. Each night she got on the Internet and read about racing events nearby. She wanted to run a few shorter races, and at least one half marathon over the summer to help get prepared for that feeling of running in a pack, to get used to the adrenaline boost so it wouldn't throw her off her stride and make her run too fast at the start.

After two weeks of this routine a sweltering day was fading into a muggy night when Ava turned on the TV to listen to the weather. She was drenched in sweat and so listless that when the phone rang she considered not answering, but on the third ring she picked it up and a slightly familiar voice said, "Hello. I'm trying to reach Ava Morrison. Is this the right number?"

Ava's brow furrowed at the man's British accent. She had a momentary impulse to hang up, just in case it was the loathsome Ainsley Wolfe. But just as quickly, she remembered the blonde good looks of David Taylor. Cautiously, she said, "This is Ava."

"Ava, this is David Taylor. We met at the department dinner last month?"

"Oh of course. I remember you."

"I hope it's all right that I called you. I got your number from the secretary at the department."

"Of course. What can I do for you?"

"Well, actually, the reason I'm calling has nothing to do with work. I just wondered if you might be free to go out for lunch or dinner sometime?"

Ava's mouth dropped open and her breaths came quickly. There was no reason she should say no. But did she want to say yes? She hesitated for a half a minute, recalling David's film star face.

"Ava? You still there?"

She gasped slightly. "Yes. Yes. Um. Yes, sure, I could go out to lunch. Or dinner. With you."

"Well great! Which would you prefer? Or we could do both if you like."

"Oh no. Just one would be good. Um . . . how about lunch?"

"Okay. Is this week good for you? How about Friday?"

Moments later Ava hung up, having agreed to meet David at the Caffe di Pagliacci in the Fan. She felt flustered and dizzy. *Gosh. What's wrong with me? I can go out with him. It's not like I'm seeing anyone else. And it's just lunch.*

She stood up and paced around her apartment, remembering how he had made her laugh at the English dinner. *This will be good for me*, she decided. *And besides*, she thought, *at least he's taller than I am. That can't be bad.*

When Friday came, Ava dressed carefully. *Attractive, but not desperate. Single, but not anxious.* Her short black skirt and sleeveless white top sent just the right casual but chic message. Should she be sending a message at all? she wondered.

When David appeared in blue jeans and a short sleeved rayon shirt the color of stormy skies Ava felt her pulse trip. What could a man like this possibly want from her? He smiled sunnily. "I'm so glad you could come," he said.

They sat at a secluded corner table and David asked Ava about her background, seeming genuinely fascinated by her story of a childhood spent traveling around the world.

"I knew there was something different about you," he said.

Ava looked at him curiously.

"When I first saw you at the dinner. It was obvious you weren't one of the usual frumpy English majors, pushing their reading glasses up on their noses and constantly quibbling about texts. When I heard you parrying Ainsley's petty jabs, I knew you had to be different."

Ava smiled despite feeling that such an obvious compliment couldn't be real. "I'm not all that unusual. Really. But you. Why did you choose to come to a school like VCU when you could have gone anywhere?"

David bent his head and looked so gravely into Ava's eyes that she expected he was about to confess some secret sorrow. "I don't want to see the America that everyone else already knows about. I want to experience the real underbelly of the country, here in the South, where the scars of the War Between the States are still visible, and, clearly, still painful for some."

"Oh." Ava sat back, nonplussed. Was he serious?

Then David unleashed his dazzling smile. "No. I can't fool you. And why should I? If I'd gone to Harvard or Columbia, or any of the top schools up North, I'd have had to work too hard to impress people. Here . . ." he chuckled slightly, "it's what you call a piece of cake. I could do it with my eyes shut."

Ava studied him, uncertain if he was joking, and, if he was, whether it was very funny. "Oh."

David sighed. "Quite frankly, I was beginning to think I'd made a mistake, until I met you."

Ava couldn't help smiling, even though one part of her mind recoiled from such an undisguised come on. "Oh really?"

"Really. When I saw you at that dinner, your natural elegance and grace, I thought, why isn't that woman a supermodel? She can't be an English professor."

Ava laughed out loud. "Boy, is this the way they do it in England? Because it's a little weak for over here."

David flashed a self-deprecating smile and reached for Ava's hand across the table. "Well, you see? That's what you can teach me. I'm a fast learner."

Ava looked at him carefully. "Yes. I'll bet you are," she said.

By the time Ava left the café she had agreed to let David take her out again on Saturday. She told herself, *okay, he's a little cocky, but who wouldn't be if they looked like him?* And she was tired of feeling alone and sorry for herself. She deserved a little fun.

In the week that followed she saw David three more times, and each time he made a point of securing a follow-up date before letting her out of sight. They went to dinner, to a movie, during which he slipped his arm lightly around her shoulders, which, strangely, didn't make her feel any warmer at all, and he surprised her by taking her to an exhibition at the Virginia Museum, allowing her a chance to show off some of her own expertise.

In one part of her mind, Ava watched all this happening with a kind of detached approval. A handsome, tall well-educated man was taking an interest in her. It was about time. But, on another level, a quiet, small, confused, and sad level, she couldn't help wondering why, if he was so wonderful, he left her so cold?

On the weekend, David arranged to pick up Ava early in the afternoon to take her to the tennis courts at Richmond U. An avid tennis player, David had insisted that Ava should learn the sport since, as he said, "Your height is a great advantage in tennis. You can dominate people from the baseline and at the net."

He seemed so eager to convince her that Ava agreed to let him try to teach her, although she had never felt drawn to the game. Everyone she knew who played it always seemed to be complaining about their game all the time, and Ava had no desire to add another frustration to her life. But, David was so insistent. And so good looking. She said yes.

Within a half hour of starting at the courts Ava was beginning to regret it. On the court next to theirs a father was trying to teach his two young children, and they kept spraying balls onto David and Ava's court. David's patience didn't seem to extend past teaching Ava.

When the little boy tripped on the court and skinned his knee and began crying, and the father led the group to the parking lot David muttered something under his breath which sounded like "about time" to Ava. She tried to concentrate on following David's directions for how to serve, volley, and hit a backhand, but she didn't seem to get the hang of it as quickly as he'd hoped.

"It's okay. It takes time. Don't worry. I'll have you hitting like Venus Williams before I'm through," David said.

"Great," said Ava, walking slowly back to the car.

* * *

On the morning of the twenty-first Ava let herself in to her apartment and Zoom scrambled over her feet and skittered across the floor to attack the phone. To Ava's dismay, the puppy had recently added ringing telephones to the list of hostile enemies, which included fire engines and ambulances, whose alarming sirens provoked his piercing howl.

"Hush! Hush, you ninny!" scolded Ava, grabbing the phone.

"Ava?"

"Nille?"

"Yeah, remember me? Blonde, witty, engaged?"

"Engaged!"

"See? You have been neglecting me. I would have told you sooner but I didn't want to leave a message and you are *never* there."

"Oh Chenille. That's wonderful. I'm so happy for you. And Howard?"

"Of course. He asked me last week."

"Wow. That's . . ." Ava took a deep breath and exhaled, sitting down before she finished with, "that's great. Really. Congratulations."

"Thanks. It's kind of amazing. We're going to wait till next year for the wedding. We want to do it in May, outside. And you have to be my maid of honor."

"Well sure." Ava punched the pillow next to her. "I'm sorry I've been so out of touch. I've been running a lot."

"Oh? I thought maybe you'd patched things up with Troy and you might have some news for me."

Ava could almost hear Chenille's dimples winking, and she felt a spasm of irritation. She didn't say anything for a moment.

"So? Ava? You still there?"

"Yeah. Still here." Ava grimaced.

"Well. What happened when you called Troy?"

Ava got up and carried the cordless over to the window. "A woman answered," she said, staring out at the street.

"Oh." Chenille hesitated. "It could have been a babysitter."

"Maybe. She sounded too old to be a babysitter."

"I see."

"Yeah. So."

"So you're telling me you still haven't talked to him since the last night of the play?"

Ava paused, pushing hard against the door to the memory of that stormy night. "That's right," she said.

"Well why not? Really, Ava. I mean, I know you were mad, but you have to get over it. So he overreacted. I bet he's really sorry now and you've made your point. He's too nice a guy to just throw away over a little misunderstanding."

Ava watched a couple walking arm in arm down the sidewalk in the glowing twilight. They were smiling at each other and laughing over something.

Ava turned away and went back to the couch, punching the pillow with renewed force.

"What am I supposed to say, Nille? I just don't know if it's worth it. Maybe it's better this way. Just forget it happened."

"Ava! What is wrong with you? Even if you never want to see Troy again you should at least give him a chance to apologize for yelling at you. You know he must feel terrible about that, and you should be big enough to forgive him."

Ava snorted. "Oh, I'm big enough. Too bad he's not."

After a moment of chilly silence Chenille said, "Okay Ava. If that's what you want. Call me if you'd like to have lunch."

Chenille's brisk tone doused Ava's petulance.

"I'm sorry Nille. I . . . I know I haven't been handling this very well. Actually, I haven't been just sitting around sulking. You remember that guy with the movie star face who was at the EM dinner?"

"You mean David Taylor? Who could forget?"

"I've been seeing him."

Chenille's stunned silence lasted about five seconds before the squeal kicked in. "And you didn't tell me? Honestly Ava! How can you be so blasé? Every woman in the department has been drooling over that man since he got here and he's been completely uninterested in anyone."

Ava couldn't help smiling, though she felt somewhat deceitful allowing Chenille to think that she had any interest in David, whose good looks Ava had decided in no way made up for his cold personality.

"Yeah, well, I would have told you, but I don't think David's really my type."

"Hah! You've got to be joking! That guy is every woman's type. He's gorgeous!"

"Yeah. He's got a pretty face. But, I don't know. He doesn't seem to have much else."

"Sheesh, Ava. If you're turning your nose up at David, maybe there's hope for Troy yet."

"Don't bring him into this. He's got nothing to do with this."

"Uh, huh? And whose fault is that?"

Ava sighed. "Nille, I'm doing the best I can. Really."

Chenille was silent for a few seconds. "Okay. That's okay. The important thing is, you're having a life. You're not moping. But don't tell me that's the best you can do. Because I know better."

Ava bit her lip and took a deep breath before she replied.

"Okay, okay. You're right, I know you're right. I'll call him. Or maybe I'll go see him at his office. I will."

"Okay. That's better," said Chenille, mollified. "Call me after you do, okay?"

"I will."

Ava hung up and sat staring at the phone. For the rest of the afternoon Ava and Zoom both kept a wary eye on the phone, but it didn't ring again until almost 5:00, and then it was Iris, calling to invite Ava to a "Midsummer's Eve" celebration at a local bar. Ava asked who else was coming and Iris said she and the other former fairies were calling most of the cast members since a lot of people had missed the cast party in the confusion of the big storm.

Hating herself for asking, Ava did. "Is Troy coming?"

"Yeah, I think so. Alex left a message on his machine. I'm sure he'll come."

It must be a sign, thought Ava. "Okay. Sounds like fun. I'll be there."

It was 7:00 that night when Troy finally got home from a long hot day on the job site where he had been forced to fill in on the hard labor because some of his steady help were on vacation. He almost ignored the light flashing on his answering machine, but the habit of hope was too strong. He pushed the button and listened to Alex inviting him to a Midsummer's Eve party at the Strawberry Street Café. Troy was so tired he considered not going until it occurred to him that Ava might be there.

He got in the shower and tried to revive himself. The hot water soothed his muscles and his mind. When he got out he slipped into a clean white t-shirt and a pair of soft worn jeans. Without thinking he sat down on his bed, laid back, and closed his eyes. *I'll just rest for a minute*, he thought.

When he opened his eyes the room was dark, the green digital display on the bedside clock read 10:15.

"Oh no!" he yelped, grabbed his wallet and keys and ran out the door.

An hour earlier Ava sat at the café bar sipping a margarita and listening to Howard and Chenille chuckling about some movie they'd been to see the night before. Ava's cheeks were tired from trying to keep the smile fixed on her face. She felt numb, depressed, and weary, and she was beginning to regret ordering a drink which went against her training regimen and her better judgment. She looked around the café again, as she had been doing for the past hour, hoping to see Troy. Not, she told herself, because she wanted to see him, but because she wanted to show him that she didn't want to see him.

"Ava? Are you okay? You look a little tired."

Ava focused on Chenille, radiant and almost oppressively cheerful, one hand on her drink, the other nestled inside Howard's.

Ava shook herself. She straightened up slightly and pushed her drink away. "Yeah. I think I'm going to have to call it a night. I'm on kind of an early schedule these days."

"When is your marathon?" asked Howard.

"The Richmond Marathon isn't till November. But I'm running in some other shorter events over the summer. It takes a lot of time to get in condition. I'm doing a half-marathon Labor Day weekend."

"Really? Where?" asked Chenille.

"Actually it's at Virginia Beach. It's called the Rock n' Roll Half Marathon, and they finish up on the boardwalk and have a rock concert and stuff."

"Wow, that sounds like fun. Maybe we can go to that one and cheer you on," said Chenille, with an inquiring glance at Howard.

"That would be nice. If you came you could watch Zoom for me while I'm running. But anyway, I think I'm going to pack it in for tonight."

Chenille scanned the café quickly, her eyes searching. Ava noticed and said, "Don't bother Nille. I already looked. He's not here. He's probably out with his new girlfriend."

"You don't know that."

"No. But neither do you." Ava slipped out of the café and went home, her sense of relief blended with disappointment.

When Troy finally arrived at the café Chenille rushed over to him and said, "Hi Troy. How have you been? You just missed Ava."

Troy sank onto a barstool wordlessly. He stayed for an hour, had a beer and made small talk with the kids from the cast and the few older members who had showed. Then, overcome with fatigue, he went home.

By the time she finished her morning run the next day Ava had decided to finish the job. Chenille might be wrong about a lot of things, but she had a point. Ava had made up her mind to make a clean break with Troy, but she felt she owed him the chance to apologize properly. So, after a quick shower and a change of clothes—nothing too flashy, but she didn't want to look forgettable either—Ava drove to Troy's office around lunchtime.

She wondered as she did so if he'd be out on a job site, but Troy had returned to his office to make some calls and eat his bagged lunch in the relative coolness. A knock on his door was so unexpected Troy put down his half-eaten tuna sandwich with some annoyance, expecting a salesman to enter. At the sight of Ava in her tangerine tank top and stretch khaki shorts, Troy's professional shell melted in a smile which didn't alter even when she opened the dialogue with the always foreboding, "We need to talk."

"I'm so glad you came. I've missed you," said Troy. "You didn't answer my calls." He stopped, noticing the veil of caution in her expression.

"Ava, I understand. I know I was out of line. I was so wrong."

"Stop it! Stop saying you were wrong!" Ava's hands trembled. Troy stared at her, his head tilted to one side, his face a crumpled map of confusion.

Ava shook her head. "You had every right to be upset. And maybe I was wrong to take Josh. But," Ava sighed, "all I know is what you said hurt me. And I can't forget it."

Troy frowned. "I don't expect you to forget it, Ava. But can't we put it behind us? You know I didn't mean it."

Ava felt the muscles in her neck stiffen. "Well, now that you mention it, that is just what I don't know." She glared at Troy. "I barely know you. And you barely know me. That's really the point isn't it? But I'm supposed to forgive and forget it when you yell at me? When you accuse me of being thoughtless and irresponsible? Of being incapable of taking care of a guppy?"

"I never said that."

"You said I couldn't take care of a goldfish. Remember?"

Troy looked down at his desk. He'd forgotten the actual words. He was beginning to realize that Ava hadn't.

Ava's voice had risen with each question and she could feel the heat in her face but she couldn't stop the anger from pouring out. For weeks she'd been fuming at the injustice of Troy's outburst and it felt good to finally let it out.

Troy sagged at his desk. In the past few weeks when he'd imagined this scene Ava had been so sweet and understanding, nothing like the aggrieved fury blazing before him.

"I . . . I don't know what to say Ava."

"Hmmph," she snorted. "What you should have said, when you opened the door, was 'Thank you Ava. Thank you for taking care of my little boy.' Why couldn't you have said that?"

Troy hung his head. "I don't know," he said softly to the floor.

Ava swallowed. "Well that makes two of us." Ava was panting slightly from the effort of venting her self-righteous wrath, but seeing Troy's shoulders slumping and the unmistakable remorse on his face, Ava felt she had better leave quickly before her resolve weakened.

"Listen, I only came here today to say I got your messages and I understand you lost your temper and you didn't mean to yell at me. And I suppose if I were a nicer person we could just forget about it and move on with whatever it was we were trying to do, which I'm not sure I knew anyway. But, I'm not that nice. Really." Ava sighed. "All I know is I don't like being yelled at. And, I don't know. I just, I just think we should forget about you and me. It's just not going to work."

Troy continued looking at the floor and Ava felt a stabbing pain in her chest. She shook her head and said quickly, "That's all I came to say."

She turned away and put her hand on the doorknob.

"Hey!" Ava's heart thudded against her chest. Troy's voice had suddenly shed its softness and Ava felt a shiver of memory so intense she almost flinched. She turned to look at him and shrank within herself. All the sunshine had gone out of Troy's face. He was standing up, his fists clenched at his side.

"Before you go, just in case you plan to walk out of here and never speak to me again, I think you should hear my side."

A spark of fury reignited inside Ava. "Well excuse me, but haven't I already heard that? You said you were sorry, poor single father, blah, blah, blah?"

Troy's fists relaxed but his expression hardened to an iceberg of disdain. "Right. Blah, blah, blah. That's how much my feelings mean to you," he said quietly. "I forgot. It's not about me is it? It's all about you. Poor little Ava. Well I'm sorry I failed to measure up to your idea of perfection, but you really scared me when you took my son. I'm sorry I yelled. I'm not perfect. I forgot that you are. That's what you really can't forgive, isn't it? Well if you're waiting for some guy who'll never make a mistake, all I can say is good luck."

Ava felt tears threatening. She yanked the door open and stormed out, slamming it behind her.

Troy pounded the desk with his fist and swore. He couldn't erase the vision of Ava glaring at him. And it only made it worse when he admitted to himself that he didn't want to forget how she looked. *God she's beautiful when she's angry*, he thought.

Ava felt so wound up after downloading her anger on Troy that she couldn't sit still. So she drove home, changed her clothes and went to the track to do one of her anaerobic threshold workouts. Once a week she varied her training to include these faster, shorter runs as part of the process of preparing her muscles for the more grueling challenge of 26.2 miles. With almost five months to train, Ava felt confident that she would be ready, but she knew that in order to get to the finish line uninjured she needed to get her body in the best shape it could be.

By concentrating on her times and focusing on the heart rate monitor, Ava managed to put Troy out of her mind for a while. But the minute she got back in her car, there he was, clouding her thoughts with regrets and something else she couldn't put a name to. Ava watched Zoom panting eagerly in the air rushing in the slightly opened window. His little body was rigid with tension and excitement.

Desire. That's what I'm feeling, Ava thought suddenly. *It's been so long I've forgotten what it felt like. And why couldn't I feel it for David?* She pounded the steering wheel in frustration. The car horn blared on the quiet street and Zoom instantly began howling. Ava swept him up in her arms and hurried him out of the car and up the stairs, hoping no one would think she was mistreating him.

"Hush you little weirdo!" she said. Zoom looked at her accusingly.

"Okay. Takes one to know one. Sorry," she added, hugging the puppy. Ava put him down on the floor and he scampered happily after a nerf ball Ava had bought to keep him amused. She watched him batting the ball and chasing after it, tossing it up in the air and snapping at it. Each time he snagged the ball he turned to Ava with the ball in his mouth and tipped his head slightly, his tail quivering like a spring.

"Yeah. It looks like fun when you do it, but I'm not sure it would work for me," she said softly.

After Ava left his office Troy threw the rest of his sandwich in the trash. He got in his truck and drove rapidly to the work site. For the rest of the afternoon he forced himself to focus on creating a natural looking artificial waterfall in a suburban yard. And if the tangerine color of the impatiens that the owner insisted on to edge the rocks reminded Troy of Ava's curves beneath her tank top, he did his best to ignore the thought.

For the next three weeks Troy became an expert at ignoring his feelings. He worked long hours and when he had no work he went out to the soccer field. With Josh out of school, Troy had more opportunities to spend time with his son, and he got in the habit of going to Josh's soccer team practices just to watch.

One sticky humid night as he sat on the metal bleachers admiring the way Josh faked his way past several defenders a woman who had been standing with a group of the waiting mothers came over and sat next to him.

"Hi," she said. Her pretty tanned face was framed with blonde streaked hair. Her pale blue eyes were friendly.

"Hello," said Troy, smiling politely.

"You're Josh's father, right?"

"That's right." Troy smiled more easily.

"I'm Justin's mom."

"Nice to meet you."

"Justin thinks Josh is the best player on the team."

Troy tried to think of something complimentary to say about Justin, but the best he could do was, "Thanks. Justin's a good soccer player too."

The woman smiled. "I'm Cathy." She held out her hand to shake Troy's. Troy shook her hand and turned back to watch Josh.

Troy wondered if it was just his imagination or if the woman really was more interested in looking at him than at her son. Then she said, "Excuse me if I'm out of line, but I was just talking with the other moms over there and they said you're a single dad."

"That's right."

Cathy simpered slightly and said, "I'm a single mom."

Troy turned and saw the needy look in her eyes and it was all he could do not to be rude. Instead he said, "That must be tough."

"It is," she gushed. "A boy needs a father."

Troy kept his eyes on Josh. He was determined not to get drawn into anything with this woman but before he could stop them the words spilled out, "They need a mother too."

Troy instantly regretted speaking. He could feel Cathy's

hope fluttering, looking for a place to land. Troy kept his mouth shut for the rest of practice, replying only with nods and grunts to the rest of Cathy's questions.

When practice finally ended at dusk, and the boys came over she said hopefully, "We should get together sometime, let the boys play."

Troy just smiled noncommittally and marched off the field with Josh looking at him curiously. When they reached the truck Josh asked, "How come you were talking to Justin's mom?"

"I wasn't talking to her. She was talking to me."

"I don't want to go play with him. He's no good."

"I know that. But I couldn't say that to her, could I?"

"No." Josh sat back against the seat. As they drove away he said, "Are we ever going to see Ava again? You said we would."

Troy sighed. "I don't know Josh. I tried to see her. But she's kind of busy."

"Doing what?"

"She's training for a marathon."

"Really!" Josh's face lit up. "That's cool. We should go watch."

"It's not for a long time. It takes a long time to get ready."

Josh frowned. "Well she can't be doing it all the time. I don't see why we can't see her sometime. Maybe she could come to one of my games."

"Maybe." Troy parked the truck and got out, hoping that Josh would forget this idea as soon as he got inside. Troy was having a hard enough time not thinking about Ava without having Josh remind him. But although once they got inside Josh quickly became absorbed in a television show about sharks and didn't mention Ava again, Troy could think of nothing else for the rest of the evening. He thought of that lonely, and admittedly attractive, single mom, who obviously wanted to get something started. And she was several inches shorter too. But she didn't make his heart race. Only Ava did.

The next day Chenille called Troy at his office.

"I don't know if you remember me. I'm Ava's friend?"

"Of course I do. You're dating Howard right? I met you at the first cast party I think." Troy's pulse picked up speed as he spoke, sensing that the call must have something to do with Ava.

"Yes. That's right. Actually, Howard and I just got engaged."

"Really! Well congratulations. That's great."

"Thank you. But that's not the reason I'm calling. I'm giving a little birthday party for Ava next week and I think she'd be really happy to see you there."

"I don't know about that."

Chenille chuckled. "Well I do. I know you guys have been going through a little thing, but I know it would mean a lot to her if you could come."

"When is it?"

"Her birthday is the 28th and she's going to be twenty-eight on the 28th so it's kind of a special birthday. It won't be a big party, but we're going to be drinking lots of champagne."

"Good plan."

"Yes. Well, Ava is my best friend, and I think she's been going through a rough time and I want this to be a happy day for her."

"If that's what you want then maybe I shouldn't come."

"Why do you say that?"

"Well, it's just the last time Ava slammed a door on me she made it pretty clear she didn't want to see me again."

"Aw, she was just letting off steam. You know how those drama queens are."

"Maybe."

"Trust me. I'll send you an official invitation, but it's going to start at eight at my place."

"Okay. Thanks for inviting me."

"Oh you have to be there. You're very important to Ava."

"Really? That's not the impression she's given me."

"Well, she's a little confused right now, but you'll see. It will all work out."

Troy smiled at Chenille's blithe confidence. "If you say so."

After he hung up Troy couldn't stop smiling. That phrase "very important to Ava" flickered in his thoughts like sunlight glinting on a mountain stream.

Chapter Fourteen

The bubbles from her second glass of champagne were just slithering down her throat when Ava looked up and saw Troy coming through the door of Chenille's apartment. She sat up quickly and sucked some of the champagne down the wrong way. Coughing and spluttering she stumbled for the kitchen where Chenille was just pulling a tray of hot mushroom hors d'oeuvres from the oven.

"Why did you invite him?" hissed Ava, as soon as she recovered her breath.

"Who?"

"You know who." Ava frowned at Chenille, who began humming as she transferred the mushrooms to a serving platter.

"Should we open another bottle of champagne before dinner do you think, or wait until dessert?" she asked.

"Hmmph. You already got David here despite what I told you. What's the big idea of asking Troy?"

"It's just a party, Ava. I invited people who like you, for whatever reason." Chenille raised her eyebrows at Ava. Ava folded her arms across her chest and leaned back against the refrigerator.

"I thought you were going to support my decision on this,

167

Nille. Now I'm going to have to be mean to him, and I don't want to be mean."

"Then don't be," snapped Chenille brightly. "Humor me, Ava. Just be polite. That's all I ask. He's a nice man. Just be nice back."

Ava scowled. "Okay, fine. Nice. The watchword for tonight."

She went slowly back into the living room and stood next to David. He quickly put his arm around her and gave a little squeeze. Ava looked across the room to where Troy was standing, talking with two women who worked in the art history department, both of them younger than Ava, and from their frequent confessional coffee chats outside Ava's door, she knew both of them were actively single. Troy was nodding and smiling as they glittered and giggled at him. Ava chafed at the sight. Troy was looking good, wearing a white shirt with the sleeves rolled halfway up his tanned, muscular arms. Black jeans hung low on his hips. He looked relaxed and happy.

"Ava! You're looking fabulous! Like a fine wine." Tim Murphy's shining red nose bobbed closer to Ava. She turned her head quickly to let his birthday kiss slide off her cheek. "Better with age," he added with a wink.

"Thanks," she said, trying not to let her irritation show. *Really*, she thought, *what was Chenille thinking inviting all these people from the play?* Then she noticed Howard holding court on the couch and she realized that Chenille had to balance more than one ego. Ava looked at Chenille, floating around the room with her canapés and cocktails, and felt a surge of gratitude to her friend for trying to lighten up the stigma of another birthday. Ava knew only too well, as a single woman, how each year the burden of proof grew heavier—having to prove to some invisible but all powerful jury that being single wasn't a sign of failure.

"Sooo Ava? What's next for the Queen of the Fairies?" Jane Murphy bobbed up next to her husband and Ava tried to run the gauntlet of personal questions which followed without actually revealing anything personal. The Murphys seemed non-plussed when Ava told them of her marathon ambitions.

"But why would you want to do that?" asked Jane. "It seems like such a lot of work and when you're all done, then what?"

"Well, I don't know. I guess I just like running," said Ava glancing around the room for some plausible excuse to escape the Murphys, who seemed to have put down roots at her side.

"Ava."

The sound of his voice made goosebumps rise on her neck. She turned and he smiled at her.

"Troy! Good to see you. How have you been?" Tim Murphy crashed into the moment with a hearty backslap for Troy and Ava stepped back quickly, letting the Murphys move closer to Troy while she edged away.

I am such a coward. Was that nice? No. That wasn't nice. But I wasn't mean, thought Ava, slipping across the room. She noticed him later watching her, but she pretended to be absorbed in the conversation of two of her colleagues. The strategy of avoidance worked well enough until Chenille announced that the sit-down dinner was ready, and then, when the chair scraping and shuffling settled Ava looked across the table and right into his eyes. He smiled again and Ava shrugged and rolled her eyes as if to say it wasn't her idea. Troy just grinned and sat down.

Throughout dinner Ava concentrated on appearing merry and bright, a picture of contentment. With David at her side, it wasn't hard. She laughed at all his jokes, even the ones she'd already heard, letting her glance slide over Troy as if he were just another face in the crowd. But at one point she noticed Chenille frowning at her and wondered if perhaps she was overdoing it. After Ava blew out the obligatory candles Chenille tapped her knife against a wine glass and the room stilled for a toast.

"When I first met Ava eight years ago at William and Mary, I was impressed by her brains, her good taste in clothes, and her incredible voice. And when she and I became friends, I learned to appreciate her dry humor, and her, um, shall we say, unique dance moves. But, as the years have gone by and we've both learned a lot about how hard it is to get ahead in this world, I've decided the main reason Ava will always be a step ahead of the pack is her legs. She's got the longest, strongest, sexiest legs of any woman I know, and if you don't believe me, go watch her this year when she'll be running again in the Richmond Marathon. To run a marathon takes a special kind of character. It takes a person who doesn't give up at the first sign of trouble, or the first touch of pain. To be a marathon runner requires not only stamina and strength, but courage, determination, and faith. There's so much more to Ava than just her lovely face or her witty repartee. So, on her twenty-eighth year in the human race, I invite you to join me in a salute to my best friend Ava: Long may she run!"

Ava blushed in the glow of cheers and applause. Ducking her head, she stole a glance at Troy and his eyes met hers with a grave, thoughtful expression. She looked away quickly, her heart skipping rapidly.

When the party wound down a few hours later and people began leaving, Ava hung close to Chenille, trying to wait out Troy, who also was lingering. She declined to leave with David, despite his insistent requests. When at last the only guests left were Iris, Alex, Howard, and Troy, Ava pulled Chenille aside and whispered, "I don't want to go home with him. Please. Can you tell Howard I'm staying here with you?"

Chenille wiggled her eyebrows. "You want me to lie for you?"

"It's my birthday."

Chenille shook her head. "Okay. I think you're nuts. But okay."

Chenille took Howard aside and explained and after a little while Howard invited the others to a nightcap at Chuggers. Troy looked at Ava but when she turned away, he started out with the others. Just before he left he walked quickly back to Ava and said softly, "Can I call you?"

Ava tensed. "I don't know. I'm going out of town to visit my parents. I'll be away for awhile."

Troy studied her face for a moment, then left without another word.

After the door closed Chenille began noisily picking up glasses and bottles. "Boy, you sure know how to celebrate," she said sarcastically.

"Nille. You know I'm trying to end it with him. You're only making it harder."

"You're the one making it harder. Why end it with the one guy who's worth your time?"

"Oh Nille. You know I respect him. He's great. And he's cute. And I know he likes me," Ava paused, unsure how to finish her argument.

"But . . . ?" Chenille, hands on hips, looked at Ava. "I'm waiting. You must have some reason for closing the door on a man like Troy. And you and David don't exactly seem to be setting the woods on fire."

"Oh David," said Ava, sighing.

"Yeah? Tell me, 'cause it's not obvious to me. What exactly is wrong with David?"

"Nothing. Nothing's wrong with David. He's perfect." Ava paused, rattling the ice cubes in her glass. "Perfect."

"And you're here with me instead of Mr. Perfect because . . . ?"

Ava shook her head. "Because I'm stupid. I don't know. I look at him and he looks great. I see us together and I know we make a good couple. He's cultured and witty."

"And tall."

"And tall." She looked at Chenille. "So why do I feel nothing for him? Nothing! He's like Prozac. I'm fine when I'm with him because I'm feeling no pain. But, you know? He doesn't make me feel alive."

"Unlike someone else."

Ava sighed. "Right."

"And we can't consider that someone else because?"

Ava hung her head. "I don't want to talk about it," she mumbled.

"Hah!" Chenille threw her hands up in the air. "There it

is! The big ugly truth. It's not that he's human. It's not that he made the mistake of criticizing you for being human too. It's not even that he's got a kid, which, admittedly, some picky females might consider a deal-breaker. No." Chenille shook her head sadly. "Ava, Ava, Ava. How can you let a little thing like that stand in your way? Good men don't grow on trees you know. And besides, lots of shorter men marry taller women all the time. Look at Tom and Nicole."

"Oh yeah, right. That worked out well."

"Okay. Bad example. How about Jerry Stiller and Anne Meara?"

"Who?"

"They're a husband and wife comedy/writing team. He played Jerry's father on 'Seinfeld?'"

"So they do comedy? So her being taller is just part of the act."

Chenille sat down, frowning. "Come on Ava. Okay, so I can't give you statistics, but I'll bet that more marriages with taller husbands end in divorce than ones with taller wives."

Ava laughed. "You're really reaching."

"Yeah, well, those shorter husbands have to toe the line, you know."

Ava fell back on the couch giggling. "I guess maybe you're right. I could be passing up the opportunity of a lifetime."

Chenille beamed. "See? I knew you'd come to see it my way."

"Or the highway."

Chenille leaned over and hugged Ava. "You know I just want you to be happy, right?"

"Yeah." Ava sighed. "Yeah I know. But, I can't forget how his face looked when he was screaming at me. It was like this whole different person. And I keep thinking, that's what can happen when you let someone into your heart—you give them the power to hurt you. And I don't want to be hurt."

Chenille's face grew serious. After a moment she said, "You know Ava, loving anyone means taking a chance. Sure, there's always the risk that you'll give your heart and someone will break it. But if you never give your heart—that's no way to avoid pain. Would you really rather live your life alone than take the chance?"

Ava sighed. "I don't know. It looks so much easier in the movies."

"That's just the special effects. In real life it's never that easy."

"What about you and Howard?"

"Hey. I waited a long time. You think that was easy?"

Ava smiled. "No." She paused. "I'm so glad you found him."

"Things will work out for you too. I know it."

"Maybe."

"Well don't give up on it. That's all I ask."

"Okay."

Later that night after sneaking back to her own apartment, where Zoom sprang joyously to meet her, Ava curled up in bed and tried to imagine a future that included Troy. And Josh. And soccer games and probably a house with a yard and neighbors and car pools and . . . she sank wearily back against her pillow. Way too complicated.

The following weekend Ava packed Zoom in the car and drove down to Charleston for her annual visit with her parents. On the seven hour drive she spent about half an hour going through the usual cycle of guilt and regret that she didn't have a closer relationship with her parents. The rest of the time her thoughts circled around memories of Troy. She remembered how he looked that night when the roof of the theatre caved in, standing there in the dank gloom, and how his face lit up when she talked with him. She remembered how his t-shirt clung to his sweaty torso during the cast soccer game, and how quickly he'd taken charge of poor Marion. She remembered the heat in his eyes and the softness of his lips when they'd gone back to his apartment that night.

Thinking of all his good qualities made Ava so depressed that she tried to stir up some anger by recalling the hurtful moment Troy had lashed out at her during the storm. But somehow, here and now, driving along in the monotony of Route 95, with the sound of his recent apologies still fresh in her mind, the memory of that brief outburst seemed far away and blunted. Maybe Chenille was right. Maybe she was being foolish not to give him another chance.

By the time Ava pulled into the narrow drive at her parents' brick row house in old Charleston she had almost made up her mind to call Troy. Once she'd gotten through the first interview with her parents.

"Ava darling, you're looking well."

Ariel Morrison floated down the curving brick steps in a yellow linen dress, her dark hair pulled back in a loose chignon, a whisper of jasmine scent preceding her. Ava embraced her mother gently. They went in together and joined Hank Morrison, reading the *Times* on a spacious lounger on the shady porch. Heavy baskets of ferns and glossy-leaved gardenias gave the space a tropical feel. Ava's father stood up and gave Ava a brief hug.

"What brings you here?" he said, the opening volley in the traditional examination.

"Oh, you know, just passing through." Ava forced a smile.

"Would you like some tea or lemonade, Ava?" Her mother hovered close by. Years as a military wife had trained Ariel to use food as a diplomatic tool. No one could be too impolite with their mouth full of cake.

"Sure, Mom, some iced tea would be nice."

Her father flapped his newspaper restlessly. Then he cleared his throat and said, "Still teaching at that school?"

"Yes, Dad. Still teaching."

Her father nodded. His own schooling had stopped nearly forty years earlier and he hadn't had much patience for it then. The subject of art history didn't fall into the narrow spectrum of topics he considered worth studying, a point of view which Ava knew all too well. "You keeping busy, Dad?"

Hank shrugged. "We do all right. Play golf three times a week. Your mother has her bridge and the garden."

"That's great. I'm glad. And your health is fine?"

"No complaints."

Ava looked out at the small immaculate formal garden below the porch. A wrought iron gate with spiky points guarded the streetside entry.

Ariel returned carrying a tray with two glasses of tea and a plate of sesame cookies. She set it down, handed one glass to Ava and the other to her husband who accepted it without a word. Then sitting back against the chintz-cushioned wicker love seat she said, "So Ava, what's new in your life? Any men on the horizon?"

Ava stifled a sigh. The inevitability of this question never diminished her distaste for it.

"No, Mom. Still waiting for the right one to show up."

Her mother's face puckered with concern. "Well, you know Ava, not everyone has to get married. Some people are better off single. There's no shame in that."

Ava stiffened. "Right. I'm not ashamed of being single, Mother."

"Of course not, dear. I never thought you were." Ariel glanced at her husband, who had retreated behind his newspaper at the first mention of marriage.

Ava tried to shift the topic, talking about the play and her new puppy, whom she'd left in the car until she could prepare her mother for the unexpected canine visitor.

"My goodness Ava. You surprise me. Shakespeare? How brave and wonderful for you. I'm sure you were excellent. You should have told us, we could have come to see you. Wouldn't that have been nice, Hank?"

Ava's father grunted from behind his newspaper. Ava felt the familiar burn of resentment on her cheeks. "Right. Well, anyway. It was fun. I met some nice people. Actually," she hesitated, then figured, *what the heck*, give her mother something to think about, "the director was, is, a very nice man. He's a single father. And he and I have been seeing each other a bit."

"Really?" Ariel sat up straighter. "Tell me about him. What does he do? He's not a theatre professional?"

"No. He's a landscape designer. He has his own company. He plays soccer." Ava hesitated. She didn't know how much more she could say about Troy without getting into his physical appearance, and she wasn't ready to deflect her mother's opinions on that topic. But Ariel was on the scent now and wasn't about to be denied.

"What's he like? Is he smart? Is he handsome?" Ariel's eyes twinkled as she asked this, as if she already knew what the answer had to be. Although Ava's mother kept a slight smile frozen on her face no matter what topic was being discussed, Ava knew from experience that the subject of appearance was one which her French mother took very seriously. It did not do to be unkempt, graceless, or inappropriate. Of course, if one were French, being *comme il faut* came naturally. But in her travels as a Marine's wife, Ariel had come to believe that in matters of style and comportment, the rest of the world had some catching up to do.

Ava took a deep breath and said, "He's smart. And nice. And I know he likes me."

"And what does he look like? Tall, dark, and handsome of course?"

Ava sat there with her mouth open. *Okay*, she thought. *A lie would be easy right about now*. She closed her mouth, lifted her chin, and smiled before she said, "Actually Mom, two out of three isn't bad."

Ariel faltered. "I'm sorry?"

Ava leaned forward and lowered her voice slightly, hoping her father was immersed in his paper. "He's handsome, Mom. And his hair is light brown. His eyes are silvery blue. And," she hesitated only a fraction before concluding, "he's five inches shorter than me."

Ariel looked stricken.

"Five inches?"

"Yup."

Ariel sat silent for a moment, absorbing this blow. Then her expression changed to one of sympathy and she said, "Oh, I'm so sorry, Ava. It must be hard for you."

It was Ava's turn to look perplexed. "I'm sorry?"

"Well, naturally you can't have a serious relationship with this man if there's that much discrepancy. You don't want to be a laughing stock at your wedding. Surely it would be better to live a life of quiet dignity alone than to spend a lifetime looking foolish?"

Ava clenched her teeth. "No. No, of course we wouldn't want that."

"I mean, I'm sure he's a perfectly nice man and there's no reason you can't enjoy his company, but it's a shame he just won't do."

Ava sat back in her chair and took in her mother, sitting docilely beside her husband, who was almost a foot taller than her. Of course, in her mother's world, size mattered. Ava wasn't so sure any more.

She had known this would be her mother's view. Why had she even brought it up? She tried to change the topic again.

"Yes. Well, anyway, in other news, I'm training for the Richmond Marathon again."

"That's nice dear. Use those lovely long legs." Ariel looked mildly toward her husband and said into the newspaper, "Isn't that nice, Hank? Ava's running another marathon."

Her father lowered his paper and looked over it at her. "The Marine Marathon?"

"No, Dad, the Richmond Marathon. The same one I ran in last year."

"Huh. You should go run with the Marines. That marathon means something."

Ava slumped back in her chair. Why did she ever imagine that visiting her parents would make her feel better? She listened to her mother rattle on about the historic preservation committee and the nuisance of horse manure in the streets from the carriage tours.

Ava could hardly wait to hear how thrilled her mother was going to be about the possibility of dog poop in her garden.

She didn't have the heart to call Troy later that night. But as she lay in bed thinking of how quickly her mother had dismissed Troy, without even meeting him, solely on the basis of his height, Ava felt a small fire of determination lit within her soul. She had been typecast all her life because of her own height, first by her mother, then by her classmates, and later by almost every man she met. Troy was the outstanding exception. He was the only man who saw into her heart and she had let him go. She longed to call him and pour out her remorse. She longed to hear the affection in his voice. But, she wondered in the dark night alone, had she waited too long?

The next morning, by the time Ava waved goodbye to her mother and climbed back in her car for the ride home, she had decided she was through being typecast.

In the week following Ava's birthday Troy spent a lot of time thinking about the persuasion problem. The more he thought about how close he'd come to persuading Ava to give her heart to him, the more Troy became convinced that this stop and start romance was turning into a chess match. He needed to plan his next move very carefully if he wanted to end up with his desired check mate.

Troy had seen the way David kept putting his arm around Ava at the party, and although he also noticed that Ava didn't seem to be reciprocating, Troy knew better than to underestimate a rival.

On the Saturday that Ava spent wishing she hadn't wasted gas and time on a trip to Charleston, Troy dialed Chenille's number.

"Troy! How nice of you to call. What can I do for you?"

Troy remembered what Ava had told him about Chenille's penchant for over-the-top romance. He was banking on it. He began by giving Chenille a brief synopsis of his efforts to woo Ava thus far. Chenille was interested to hear his version of events, having heard the mirror-version from Ava already.

"So, what I want to know," said Troy, after he'd finished his account of the most recent brush-off, "is, what do I have to do to get Ava to give me another chance?"

"Hmm. Well, that's a great question. And I really want to see you succeed, because, quite frankly Troy, I think you're the right man for Ava."

"Well, thanks. I wish she'd see it that way."

"Hmm. Here's the thing. I don't think a simple speech is going to do the job at this point. You two have come far enough that it's going to have to be something more dramatic."

"You mean, like a gesture?"

"Yeah. But it can't be something ordinary, like flowers or balloons."

"Or a singing telegram."

"Definitely not. No. But, you know, something dramatic, something public, something that tells the whole world that Ava is the woman you love. That's what you need."

"Like a sky writer?"

"Maybe. I don't know, then you could get screwed by the weather, or she might not see it. But, that's the right direction to go in I think. You need to break through her defenses and overwhelm her with passion. Show her you're serious."

"Huh. That's a tall order."

"Yeah. Well, so is Ava."

Troy smiled. "I guess you're right. Okay, I'll think of something."

"I know you will. Good luck."

"Thanks Chenille."

Troy hung up the phone and gazed around his apartment without thinking. His glance fell on the large mock-up of the Blue Rose Landscape logo. Troy stared at it, recalling how he'd explained the reason behind the name to Ava long ago when they'd first met. As he stared, an idea took shape in his mind and he started feeling more optimistic than he had for months.

Chapter Fifteen

O most courageous day! O most happy hour!

At 5 A.M. on the Sunday before Labor Day, the day of the Rock n' Roll Half Marathon, Ava got up and pulled back the curtains to watch the sunrise beginning over the Atlantic. At this quiet hour the beach was empty and the air was still cool. Ava inhaled deeply, glad she had left Zoom with Chenille and Howard last night so she could concentrate on the race.

She stretched, ate her power breakfast and headed down to the registration area at the Pavilion Convention Center. The weather was perfect. Several thousand runners were already milling around. Ava glanced briefly at the small crowd of spectators gathered at the starting line. A much bigger crowd would wait at the halfway mark. Chenille and Howard had promised to wait there, with Zoom on a leash, to cheer as Ava went by. Ava breathed deeply as she strapped on her number. She slipped into the center of the throng of runners. As usual there was a staggering variety. Some had gray beards and stringy arms, some were tanned and taut, lycra-clad and leggy. A few were chubby. Ava felt a swell of compassion for the earnest hopes of all these strangers. Maybe they were running to escape their problems too. For a few hours at least, they would all share the same problems, the unforgiving challenge of the pavement, mile after mile.

Then the gun sounded and the pack began trotting down 19th Street, a bobbing sea of colored nylon, pumping arms and pattering sneakers.

For the first few miles Ava felt no pain. She was almost carried along by the momentum of the pack, the camaraderie of the event. The flat route took them down Pacific Avenue, past a lot of the beach hotels and out along General Booth Boulevard before stretching out around Camp Pandelton. Crossing the Rudee Inlet Bridge Ava noticed the early morning surfers on the ocean side, while fishing boats and glamour yachts bobbed in the harbor on the other side. By the time they crossed the inlet bridge the second time and were heading back in toward the city, the pack had stretched to breaking and the runners were more loosely connected. Ava jogged behind a well-knit core of younger women who she guessed might be on one of the college track teams because of the disciplined way they traded the lead in their little group. Ava paced herself some ten yards behind them.

When they came to the turn at the halfway mark Ava looked into the crowds of cowbell-ringing supporters lining the streets. At first she thought she'd missed Chenille, but then she saw a tiny animal lunging at the passing runners and she recognized Zoom, just barely restrained by the leash Chenille was tightly gripping.

"Woooo Ava! Looking good!" Chenille yelled. Ava smiled and waved as she went by. Zoom yapped furiously. The moment passed in a blur of bright balloons, cheering children, and sunshine, and the thought flashed through Ava's mind that she had already run six miles and she wasn't at all tired yet.

Then, unexpectedly a darker shadow crossed her mind as she had a momentary thought of what would happen when the race was over. The emptiness of that vision rose unbidden in Ava's mind and she felt a sudden chill. She slowed her pace slightly and concentrated on matching her footsteps to the rhythm of the girls ahead of her. *Don't think about tomorrow*, she told herself. *Don't think about tonight. Just keep moving.*

As the sun rose higher in the sky the temperature rose with it. The gaps between clots of runners grew wider and the less fit slowed, gasping and cramping by the wayside. Ava welcomed the heat. The hot sun felt strong and vital on her skin. She felt like she could run forever.

This euphoria gave way to a more oppressive weariness after the tenth mile, however. Ava pounded along Atlantic Avenue, where scores of race support staff offered bottles of water to the runners. She was shaking her head to wave them off when she heard a collective bubble of amusement from the girls ahead. At first she thought they must be chuckling at the huge fifteen-foot tall beach ball sculptures that decorated a vacant lot on the strip. But then she looked farther up and saw as she went past a makeshift billboard by the side of the boardwalk. It was about ten feet across and eight feet high, mounted on a wooden frame like a portable stage set. A border of big blue roses framed the sunny sign on which someone had painted in ornate script: *When fleet compete upon the street/ or on the measured mile,*

That was it. Ava puzzled over this as she ran but very soon the girls emitted another collective giggle and another similar style sign came into view. It read: *My weary legs feel stronger, because of Ava's smile.*

Ava stumbled and nearly fell. She recovered quickly, her heart pounding a strange tattoo out of synch with her feet. It couldn't be a coincidence. Ava was not a common name. She ran on, her thoughts racing even faster than her feet.

Perhaps five minutes later another shriek went up from the girls. Ava looked and the next billboard read: *While other runners falter, and slowly fall behind,*

Ava tried not to smile. The Burma Shave rhythm of the meter was beginning to get in her head. She found herself trying to guess the next rhyming phrase, but when it came into view a few minutes later Ava's throat tightened as she read it. *My pace will never alter, for Ava's on my mind.*

Ava ran on, shivers of anticipation clashing strangely with the sweat running down her back. She tried not to let the image of Troy cloud her mind, but she couldn't stop it. His words were in her head. She knew it had to be him, and the thought made her dizzy. A cheer from the girls brought Ava back to the moment. The next sign read: *Some may run for pleasure, and some to win a prize.*

Ava suddenly wondered if Troy was waiting at the finish line. And her paced slowed slightly as she remembered the strange woman's voice who had answered the phone. What if all of this was some hoax? What if there was another girl named Ava? Ava ran on in a state of total emotional confusion. The next sign didn't make it any better. *I run in hopes of catching a glance from Ava's eyes.*

While the squadron of girls speculated about the mystery of the signs, Ava tried unsuccessfully not to. If Troy had made them, then he must have some reason. And if someone else had made them, well, Ava didn't want to believe that. She wanted Troy to be the one. And as she recognized this desire, the heartfelt longing to have Troy back in her life, a funny feeling rose in her chest and she turned her head and saw Troy, dressed in runner's clothes, complete with a marathon number, jogging up the boardwalk to catch up to her.

He pulled up next to her and they ran without speaking for perhaps a hundred yards. Then she said, "What are you doing here?"

He said, "I don't like to talk when I'm running." Ava stared at him for half a minute. Then she stopped abruptly.

Troy stopped a few paces ahead and trotted back to where Ava stood, hands on her hips, trying to glare at him but not quite succeeding.

"Well?" she said. Seagulls wheeled and screeched high above. Waves crashed against the beach behind her.

"Well what?" he asked, running in place.

Ava flung her arms skyward. "You know what. What's with the signs? What do you want?"

Troy stopped running and looked at Ava gravely and said, "Isn't it obvious?"

"Not to me. The only thing that's obvious to me is that I'm five inches taller than you and I don't think you can handle that."

Troy frowned. "You think you're taller than me?"

Ava laughed. "You hadn't noticed?"

Troy smiled gently and said, "No, Ava. The problem isn't that you're too tall for me. The problem is that I'm too short for you."

"I don't think of you as short."

"Well I don't think of you as tall, either."

"Oh really? And just how would you describe my height?" said Ava, folding her arms and looking at Troy skeptically.

Troy met her gaze serenely, and hesitated only a moment, like a man measuring the distance before leaping from one tall building to another.

"I think you have the proportions of a goddess," he said.

"Hah!" Ava couldn't hold back her bark of laughter. "Boy. Did you rehearse that?" she asked, smiling despite herself.

"Yeah," said Troy, smiling back. "What do you think?"

Ava shook her head and looked at him. "It needs work," she said. "But I guess it will do for now."

They looked at each other for a moment in the bright sunshine. A quartet of puffing joggers ran past them.

"Are there any more of those signs?" Ava asked.

"There might be."

Ava pursed her lips to keep from smiling as she started jogging ahead. Troy quickly fell into step beside her as they headed into the last mile and a half stretch of the marathon. For several minutes Ava kept her eyes focused ahead, listening to the sound of their footsteps beating in perfect time. Then she saw it.

A hundred yards ahead she could see the now familiar

billboard outline at the thirteen-mile mark. A cluster of people were gathered around it and she couldn't make out the writing until they were almost upon it. Then she read: *If you'll forgive me Ava, I'll never leave your side.*

Ava's throat tightened and she felt tears stinging her eyes but she kept running, not daring to look at Troy who was matching her step for step. Within a minute she heard the rising murmur of a much larger group gathered by another billboard. She stole a brief glance at Troy, but his eyes were focused ahead. She turned to read the sign. It was larger and more ornate than the previous ones, as if to underscore its message.

I'll wait until the day when you consent to be my bride.

Ava gulped. So there it was. In bold print for all the world to see.

In a daze she noticed that TV crews were positioned by the billboard, scanning the runners passing by, clearly hoping to catch the romance in motion.

Ava looked at Troy and saw the love in his eyes and she felt a joy unlike anything she'd ever known. She reached out her hand and he took it and they ran on holding hands for the last hundred yards until they crossed the finish line where they stopped and fell into each other's arms. Cameras flashed and popped around them. Several reporters thrust microphones at them but Troy, turning his head aside for just a moment, said, "Please. Could we have a few minutes?"

He looked at Ava and she shook her head, smiling.

"Is that a no?" he asked apprehensively.

"No," she said. "It's not a no." She looked down at the ground for a moment, then at the crowd of people watching them. Then she looked back at Troy, waiting, still holding her hand.

"It's up to you, Ava," said Troy softly. "What do you want?"

Ava bit her lip to keep from smiling. At that moment Josh burst through the crowd with Chenille and Zoom right behind him.

"Dad! Dad! Ava's got a puppy! See? She's got just what I've always wanted!"

Josh lifted Zoom and the puppy wriggled happily in his grasp.

Troy looked Ava and said, "Yup. She's got just what I've always wanted too."

Ava laughed and pulled Troy closer until she could whisper for his ears only, "Are you sure you can handle it?"

Troy grinned and squeezed her closer as he whispered, "I can hardly wait."